The gun blasted.

Hudson's chest constricted. Had she been hurt?

"Vienna!" he called.

She pushed herself up onto her knees. Her fleece pullover showed a trace of red seeping through, but it wasn't gushing. "I'm okay."

Something crashed against Hudson's back, sending him staggering into the desk. He shoved off from the wood, spinning to land a punch in the attacker's stomach. Vienna dived for the gun the assailant had left on the ground. As her hands latched around it, the man launched himself at Hudson, tackling him to the ground. Vienna rolled out of the way, but the second man fired at her. She screamed.

"Get out of here!" Hudson grunted, struggling to keep his own weapon out of his attacker's grasp. They rolled across the ground until Hudson finally landed on top and smashed the butt of his gun into the man's face. He shoved to his feet. "Vienna, run!"

Kellie VanHorn is an award-winning author of inspirational romance and romantic suspense. She has college degrees in biology and nautical archaeology, but her sense of adventure is most satisfied by a great story. When not writing, Kellie can be found homeschooling her four children, camping, baking and gardening. She lives with her family in western Michigan.

Books by Kellie VanHorn

Love Inspired Suspense

Fatal Flashback
Buried Evidence
Hunted in the Wilderness
Dangerous Desert Abduction
Treacherous Escape

Visit the Author Profile page at LoveInspired.com.

Treacherous Escape

KELLIE VANHORN

LOVE INSPIRED SUSPENSE

INSPIRATIONAL ROMANCE

LOVE INSPIRED® SUSPENSE
INSPIRATIONAL ROMANCE

ISBN-13: 978-1-335-59802-8

Treacherous Escape

Copyright © 2024 by Kellie VanHorn

Recycling programs
for this product may
not exist in your area.

For questions and comments about the quality of this book, please contact us at CustomerService@Harlequin.com.

® is a trademark of Harlequin Enterprises ULC.

Love Inspired
22 Adelaide St. West, 41st Floor
Toronto, Ontario M5H 4E3, Canada
www.LoveInspired.com

Printed in Lithuania

MIX
Paper | Supporting
responsible forestry
FSC® C021394

And we know that all things work together for good to them that love God, to them who are the called according to his purpose.
—*Romans* 8:28

For Mom and Dad, who taught me about Jesus,
and who let me read at the dinner table even though
they probably weren't supposed to.
Thank you for always believing in me. I love you.

With heartfelt gratitude to my editor, Katie Gowrie;
my agent, Ali Herring; and critique partners,
Kerry Johnson and Michelle Keener.
I couldn't ask for a better team!

ONE

Vienna Clayton's footsteps echoed in the empty hallway as she carried her laptop to the conference room at the far end, past darkened labs on one side and floor-to-ceiling windows on the other. Normally the glorious view of Lake Superior made her feel relaxed, but tonight the dying sunlight deepened the blue of the lake into an ominous black, and the growing wind outside whipped the water into choppy waves.

Dr. Kevin Glickman, her employer and the founder of BioMed Research Lab, glanced up from his notepad when she entered the room. He'd created the facility nearly two decades earlier to focus on the rising problem of antibiotic-resistant superbugs, an area she'd focused on in her postdoc. "Vienna, thank you for staying late," he said. "I didn't want to risk extra ears overhearing your lab results. I'm sure you understand."

"Completely." After what had happened at the small pharmaceutical company over the past few years, she'd done everything she could to protect her data, too. She set the laptop on the table and took a minute to plug it into the overhead projector.

The lab had suffered a major fire only two years earlier. They'd lost a lot of equipment, years of data and, worst of all, one of her colleagues had died. Since then, Bios Phar-maTech and a few other competing small companies had gotten the jump on some of their possible drugs, beating them to much-needed government grants. Dr. Glickman didn't share much about the company's financial status, but if BMRL didn't get a grant soon, Vienna suspected layoffs would be heading their way. Possibly even bankruptcy.

But not with the good news she had to share today. She tapped a few buttons on the keypad and allowed herself a small smile as her presentation appeared on the big screen. God had been so good, blessing her work, and now they'd be able to use it to help the entire world fight back against deadly infections.

"I think you'll be very excited about this data, Dr. Glick-man. The newest formula I tested, coded BMRL 817, not only killed MRSA and CRE *in vitro*, but there were also no negative side effects. With these data, we could—"

She broke off, startled, as someone appeared in the open doorway.

Someone clothed entirely in black, their face concealed beneath a ski mask.

Her mouth fell open, but before she could speak, a flash of light burst from a gun in the person's hand. The report boomed a fraction of a second later. Dr. Glickman slumped forward against the table, immobile. Liquid red spread across the surface.

Vienna screamed as her heart leaped up into her throat. Every nerve fired at full blast, shooting adrenaline through her system. She lunged for the floor, throwing herself beneath the table, even though a tiny rational voice in the back of her mind told her there was nothing to stop the shooter from bending down.

But the assailant—a man, judging by his height and

shape—didn't fire again. Instead, his footsteps thudded on the carpeted floor as he ran around the table. Vienna could barely breathe as she bolted for the open door, half expecting to feel a bullet hit her back, but when she chanced a glance back, the man was busy unhooking her laptop.

As she ducked out into the hall, static crackled from a radio and the man's voice carried out of the room. "Target one is dead. Laptop acquired. Target two is running. All units move to intercept. We need her alive."

Dead. Dr. Glickman was *dead*. Horror and fear ballooned inside her chest, bubbling up into her esophagus. But then the man's other words hit home.

All units move to intercept.

She had to run.

Footsteps pounded behind her from more than one direction. She ran past the conference room and took a right, following the hallway as it wrapped around the building. The emergency stairs were halfway down, if she could only reach them. A door slammed somewhere up ahead, and more pounding came from in front of her. Someone else had beaten her to the stairs.

Where else to go?

"Stop!" The man in black appeared around the bend, her silver laptop tucked in one hand, the gun in the other.

Panic clawed at her insides, but she willed herself to think. He'd said they wanted her alive, so he couldn't just shoot her. Not to kill, anyway.

Her frantic gaze landed on the glass windows in front of her. On the other side, orange metal railings rimmed the big concrete deck overlooking Lake Superior. Picnic tables provided the chance to sit outside during employee breaks, but now that deck might offer her only escape route.

She dashed forward, lunging for the door a few feet

away, and pushed outside. Warning shots rang out behind her, shattering one of the glass panes and bouncing off the concrete. The wind tugged at her white lab coat and tore strands of her hair loose from its bun. She reached the railing, clasping her hands around the cold metal, damp from mist off the lake.

A dozen feet below, waves frothed at the rocky edge of the water. To the right, a wooden dock jutted out into the lake, a lone boat bobbing against the side. With BMRL's location on an isolated section of coastline north of Grand Marais, Minnesota, boating to work instead of driving was common. She didn't have her own boat yet, but Dr. Glickman did.

She swallowed. He wouldn't need it now.

After hoisting herself up, she climbed over the deck railing and dangled from the metal bar. Hard rocks stared at her from eight feet below where she hung. Her knees ached just thinking about the drop, but at least the dress code at BMRL was casual. She'd worn hiking boots, jeans and a pullover on this chilly spring day. Bracing for impact, she let go of the railing as voices sounded overhead.

Her feet slammed onto the rocky ground, sending a jolt of pain through her legs. She stumbled forward, nearly going down, but managed to keep upright as she scrambled for the dock. A horrible thought struck her as she raced over the damp, slick wood. What if Dr. Glickman had his keys in his pocket?

She clambered over the gunwale into the twenty-foot boat and ducked beneath the center console as more warning shots rang out from the balcony. Wood chips flew from the dock, pelting the side of the boat and landing in her hair. Keeping low, she scanned the console and let out a relieved breath when she spied the keys dangling from a hook under the canopy top. *Thank You, Lord.*

The engine kicked on right away as she cranked the keys in the ignition. A faint burning odor from the exhaust mingled with the scent of rain carried on the breeze. With the way this wind was blowing, the boat would drift away from the dock as soon as she untied the lines. She crouched behind the cover of the center console and worked her way to the bow line first, tugging the knot loose from the mooring. But as she turned for the stern, a dark form dropped over the railing of the deck, and the man who'd chased her earlier raced across the rocky shore.

Heart in her throat, Vienna leaped for the stern line and yanked it loose, pushing the boat off from the dock. The wind caught the vessel and pulled it away from shore as she turned back to the console. At least she wouldn't end up beached on the rocks. She moved the lever to engage the engine and maneuvered the boat out into the water. Her pursuer ran to the end of the dock, firing shots at the boat's stern, joined by another man on the deck. A third came dashing out an exit on the building's ground floor, but their shots fell short in the frothy waves.

Relief coursed through her system. As long as they didn't know where she lived, she could head north up the coastline, get to safety and notify the authorities using her landline. Her cell was back in the lab, along with all her personal identification, but there was no turning around now.

With this growing wind and darkness, the lake wasn't the safest place to be, but thankfully she had years of experience on the water from growing up in coastal Maine. In grad school at MIT in Boston, she'd tried talking her ex-husband into getting a boat when they graduated, but he wasn't interested. In fact, that pretty much described their

entire brief relationship. Not interested. Not in her, anyway. He'd been plenty interested in his coworker, though.

Her stomach soured, but she forced her concentration
back to steering the boat. At least the coast offered more
protection than the open waters of Lake Superior would.

As she turned the boat around, the roar of another engine
layered in with the sound of hers and the blustery wind.
Her breath caught. She glanced back toward shore, shov-
ing hair out of her eyes.

Another boat appeared around the promontory, having
come from a hidden spot around the side of the lab building. It pulled up next to the dock, picked up the three men,
then turned. Heading straight for her.

For a second she couldn't think straight, couldn't even
see, as terror tugged her mind into a black abyss. She
cranked the wheel, steering the boat away from her pursuers. Where to go now? Home was out of the question. There
was nowhere to hide along the open coast. And if their
speedboat was faster than Dr. Glickman's fishing vessel, as
it appeared to be, she'd never lose them on the open water.

What about the small islands dotting the coastal waters
of this section of the lake? Not as far as Isle Royale, but the
ones closer inland? She hadn't lived here long enough to
explore much of the area, but she'd been out to the islands a
few times. Could she outmaneuver them and hide in a cove?

It might be her only chance.

Scanning the boat's instrument panel, she found the
chartplotter and flipped it on, then tugged on a life jacket
while she waited for it to load. It'd be more comfortable to
take off her lab coat, but between this wind and the lake
spray, she'd be chilled to the bone before long. Better to
keep it on. Sonar readings popped up a few seconds later,
showing schools of fish beneath the hull and the depth of

the bottom. At least she wouldn't be going in completely blind.

A wave slapped the side of the boat and sent frigid spray up into her face. Chill wind nipped her cheeks, churning up the waves. Before long these waters would be recklessly dangerous. With the sun slipping behind the trees in the west, she'd soon be draped in total darkness. Maybe it would help her hide.

But as she headed east across the growing swells and the other boat followed, her stomach twisted. Was she sailing into an early grave?

If this wind was any indicator, it was going to be a whopper of a storm later tonight.

Hudson Lawrence slowed the engine of his National Park Service patrol boat and let it bob in the waves for a few minutes as he scanned the coastline of Isle Royale with a pair of binoculars. The wind had been building slowly over the course of the afternoon. The sun had slipped behind a growing blanket of clouds that blocked the nighttime stars. Moonlight still streaked across the water, but it was only a matter of time before the incoming stormfront consumed the moon, too.

Time to end this patrol. Other than the slap of waves against the hull and the snap of his jacket in the wind, the night was quiet. He'd made it through his full route along the island's northwestern coastline, even stopping at Todd Harbor to chat with a nice couple who'd sailed over from Michigan's Upper Peninsula a few days prior. They'd been aware of the forecast and had taken adequate safety precautions. They'd be fine. As would the kayakers at Huginnin— their red and yellow vessels had been dragged well up onto the beach when he'd passed by on his return.

As he stowed the binoculars back into their protective case, a long beep sounded on his radio, followed by a recorded message from the National Weather Service. "Surf advisory for Lake Superior. North winds building to twenty to thirty knots, potential gale force gusts to thirty-five knots. Waves increasing from five to nine feet, possibly up to thirteen."

His teeth clenched. Five feet? No problem. Thirteen? It'd get ugly out here later. Good thing he didn't have far to go.

He reengaged the engine, savoring the feel of the boat gliding up and over the rising swells. It felt good to be back out here, after the long winter on the mainland in Houghton with the other full-time rangers. He'd helped with the winter wolf study, but that had still left too many weeks of desk work before the island opened for the summer season. When he was here, he could immerse himself in nature and the outdoor work he loved. Here, he could almost forget.

The boat cut across the growing whitecaps as he steered for home. A few more miles and he'd make the turn south through North Gap and into Washington Harbor, where the water would be calmer. Then into Windigo, where he'd been stationed for this season. All the seasonal employees wanted Rock Harbor—he'd passed a summer there himself, after his wife died—but there was something special about this end of the island. More remote, more backpackers and less day-trippers. A place to test yourself without life's comforts getting in the way. God took all that away sooner or later, anyway.

He swallowed the bitter taste in his mouth and focused on guiding the boat up and down each rising swell. As he came around the headland, something flashed in the corner of his eye—moonlight on the water? There it went again, a light flickering out on the lake to the west. Too far north to be from one of the small islands guarding Washington Harbor. And the ferry that carried visitors to Minnesota had left hours ago. It wouldn't be making a return trip in this weather.

Reducing speed, he let the boat drift for a minute as he tugged the binoculars back out. It was hard to tell in the growing darkness, but from the way the light cut erratically in and out, it looked like another boat heading for Isle Royale. Hudson stowed the binoculars again and picked up his onboard radio.

When the dispatcher picked up, he identified himself and provided his location, then said, "There's a light on the water, bearing 286 degrees, approximately two hundred meters away. Could be a small watercraft in trouble. Going to check it out before I head in."

"Copy, Ranger Lawrence. You hear the advisory? Be careful."

"Will do." He clicked off and then turned the boat toward the light. The waves grew choppier as he headed away from the protection of the island, until he was forced to cut his speed or risk flipping over. It'd be even worse out on the open water between here and Minnesota—Lake Superior was known for its changeable, hazardous conditions. So how had that boat made the crossing in this wind?

As he approached, the vessel's outline became visible as a dark mass surrounding a center console light, not unlike his own patrol boat. He flipped on his search lights, shining them in the direction of the other boat. It changed course, veering away from intercepting him to cut northeast. A difficult heading with these waves. His stomach clenched as the boat hit a bigger wave, tilted precariously at the top and then slid back down safely. What was the pilot thinking?

The same swell met his boat head-on, lifting the vessel

up and over with a spray of freezing water. That one had to be close to eight feet, just on the border of safe wave heights for his twenty-four-foot vessel. And the other boat looked even smaller.

He flipped on his radio and announced his identity on the frequencies typically used by boaters. No response. Maybe that shouldn't be a surprise given the challenge of controlling a boat out here, but then why was the pilot actively moving away from him?

Frowning, he turned north, moving to intercept. Over the top of his console, the wind whipped the small flags on their poles with a steady clinking sound. Moonlight danced on the frothy surf and the air smelled of coming rain. Time to try the old-fashioned way of communicating. After opening a compartment near his feet, he yanked out a megaphone. As his boat drew closer to the other one, he pointed the megaphone toward the other vessel.

"National Park Service. Do you need help?" His voice boomed across the water, but the other boat kept on its heading, tilting precariously with each swell. Could the navigator not hear him?

He shook his head, stuffing the megaphone back at his feet, and gripped the wheel tighter. Even with his training, it was getting dangerous out here. The other boat swerved precariously, angling its beam the wrong direction as it crested the wave. Almost as if the driver was distracted— or worse, incapacitated. Hudson's shoulders tensed.

For a second the boat hung on top of the crest as if suspended in midair, then toppled, rolling over on its beam and vanishing on the other side of the wave.

Adrenaline zipped through every nerve in his body as he pushed his boat forward through the waves. The capsized vessel reappeared a moment later on the other side of a wave. The canopy roof was still visible above the water, but the hull was filling fast and would soon tip over completely.

Where was the pilot? And had anyone else been on board?

He scanned the water with his floodlights. *Please, God, help me find whoever was on that boat before it's too late.*

The breath gushed from his lungs as a head popped to the surface twenty feet away from the capsized vessel. Silver reflective strips gleamed against a neon yellow life jacket. It was impossible to tell from here whether the victim was conscious. He brought his boat as close as he dared, then let the engine idle as he called out, "Hey! Hey, there!"

At first there was no response, but then a head turned in the water, and his floodlights caught the wide eyes and pale face of a woman. She stared at him for a second, then covered her face as a spray of water came off the next wave. He had to get her out before she crashed into the capsized boat. Or his.

He unhooked a ring buoy and tied one end tightly to the inside of the gunwale. The next wave brought her closer, and he yelled again, "I'm throwing you a life preserver, okay?"

She waved her arms at him, which hopefully meant she understood, and he heaved the ring across the gap between them. It splashed into the water a few feet away. The woman swam over and clung on to the ring. Hudson hauled the line back in, pulling her toward his boat. When she was a few feet away, he braced his legs against the gunwale and leaned out. She held up a wet, shaking hand, and he clasped on to it, doing everything in his power to keep her from being dashed into the side of the boat by the waves.

When he could get a hand beneath her other arm, he hoisted her up and over the gunwale, staggering backward beneath her weight as the boat rocked. She slid into a soggy heap on the deck.

"Here." He helped her back up and guided her across

the rolling deck toward the bench seats under the console canopy. Her teeth chattered like they'd break and fall out of her mouth, and her clothing—a long white coat over blue jeans—was icy cold and dripping. They needed to get moving back to safety before his boat rolled over, too. After fishing in a compartment, he tugged out a thick wool blanket and wrapped it around her shoulders. "Keep this around you. I've got to get us off the open water, and then we'll get you warmed up. Were you the only one on that boat?"

She turned a pale face up to him, her brown eyes wide, her dark hair wet and clinging to her cheeks and neck. She managed to nod, but her body looked so stiff she might topple over any minute. He frowned but turned back to the steering wheel. There was nothing more he could do out here, with the wind gusting harder and the waves increasing. Overhead, the clouds now stretched most of the way across the sky. Far in the distant west, faint traces of lightning flickered over the lake, and thunder rumbled.

He guided the boat toward the small islands dotting the harbor entrance. The surf had risen in the half hour since he'd first come out here. With each rise and fall of the boat, cold water sprayed across the console's glass. It took all his concentration to keep them from veering the wrong direction and capsizing. Next to him, the woman sat shell-shocked and silent. With the way she was clutching white-knuckled to the bars next to her seat, at least he didn't have to worry about her falling out.

Keeping one hand firmly on the wheel, he used the other to call the dispatcher on the radio and update her on the status of the capsized vessel and the victim. The rangers would have to wait for the weather to clear before attempting to recover the lost boat.

ETA into Windigo, thirty minutes. At least there shouldn't be any other traffic in the harbor.

But the thought had barely flicked through his brain when the roar of another engine mingled with the moaning wind.

The woman, who'd been so silent since he'd pulled her from the frigid waters, let out a sharp cry. "They found me!" she gasped.

What…? He followed her gaze to the west, where the visibility was now almost completely obscured by darkness and the even darker bank of low-lying clouds. But the approaching twin floodlights were unmistakable. Someone else was out here on the lake.

"Go!" she urged, struggling to rise from her seat as if she were going to take over piloting.

He held up his hand. "Whoa, you need to stay put. Let me handle this." Frowning, he picked up the radio and set it to the most common boating frequency as the other vessel drew closer.

She whimpered. "No, you don't underst—"

"This is National Park Service patrol boat *Elizabeth Kemmer*," he said into the radio, cutting her off. "Coordinates four seven decimal nine zero north, eight nine decimal two three west. Please identify yourself."

No answer came through the crackling static.

He crammed his finger down on the button again. "Repeat, this is National Park—"

A series of sharp cracks sounded over the water, followed seconds later by answering pings across the boat's hull. It took a moment for his brain to clear from the shock enough to register what was happening. Someone in the other boat was shooting at them.

TWO

Vienna screamed, slipping off her seat and down onto the deck next to the ranger's legs. She tucked herself into a ball, wrapping her arms over her head. Every muscle ached, and she was so cold her bones felt like they'd been dunked in liquid nitrogen. She half expected them to shatter, but everything stayed intact. For the moment.

"They're firing at us!" the ranger exclaimed. Something—shock or indignation, maybe—tinged his words. He glanced down at her, his forehead crinkling. "Hold on to something!"

She pried her hands off her head and wrapped her fingers around a metal bar running beside the seat. The boat rose over another crest then plunged in a sickening drop on the other side, which sent a spray of water pelting in beneath the console roof. What little she could see of the approaching vessel faded into shadow as the moon vanished behind the forerunner of the clouds.

More gunshots sounded across the water, and the boat swerved suddenly to the right. Vienna slid across the wet floor, and she tightened her grip on the metal bar. Her fingers were so numb with cold she could barely feel them.

"I'm cutting our lights," the ranger said. "We'll try to lose them in a cove."

For a moment she couldn't tell the difference as the other boat's floodlights bore down on them, but then he turned their vessel and suddenly they were bathed in darkness. Their boat sliced across the waves at a different angle now, tipping them precariously as they crested the next wave. Was that how her boat had flipped? The sickening feeling in her stomach seemed to think so, but she couldn't remember exactly how it had happened. Only that she'd hit freezing cold water and thought that was the end, until the park ranger had rescued her.

Another shiver wracked her body as the boat kept turning, heading east now as best she could tell. It was utterly disorienting. She wanted to twist around to check for the other boat, but her body was too numb to cooperate. Even her head felt like a buoy tossed by the waves.

And that image of Dr. Glickman, slumped across the table, dead… It wouldn't leave her alone. No matter how hard she squeezed her eyes shut, she could still see him. Acid churned in her stomach.

For several minutes the boat zigzagged through the surf along the coastline, until the ranger made a hard turn. Suddenly the wind died down. The waves lapped gently against the side of the hull. Soothing, almost. A cliff wall rose nearby, explaining the lack of wind. The ranger cut the engine, and the night grew quiet except for the soft sloshing of the waves.

He stood still as a statue, watching the water behind the boat's stern. She shifted, trying vainly to force her lifeless limbs to stand up.

"Shh," he whispered.

Raindrops started to fall, pattering lightly on the canopy over her head and the deck around her. An engine's roar cut through the night, freezing the breath in her lungs. *Please don't let them find us, Lord.*

Keep going, she silently urged, straining to listen. The roar grew in volume, then started to fade as the other boat passed by. She sagged back against the bench. The ranger urged their vessel forward on the quietest, slowest engine setting.

A few minutes later, he slowed the engine to an idle. She waited in shivering silence as he hoisted an anchor over the bow and tugged the chain to make sure it was secure. Wet hair clung tenaciously to her cheeks, and she brushed it back. Where were they?

In a moment the ranger came back to her, crouched down and spoke in a whisper. "I can't risk entering the harbor yet or they might see us, so we'll stay here for a few hours until they're gone."

A few hours? In these dripping, cold clothes? A shiver wracked her spine so hard she felt like she was convulsing.

"Hey," he said, "hang in there. As soon as I get this dinghy inflated, we'll go to shore and build a fire to get you warmed up. Why don't you take this to keep some of the rain off when we leave the cover of the canopy?" He tugged the ball cap off his head and handed it to her, then helped her get to her feet and sit on the bench seat again. He went into the bow, where he rummaged through some compartments. After pulling out a small foot pump and a rolled-up bundle, he unfurled the raft on the front deck. "What's your name?"

"Vi… Vienna… Clayton," she said through chattering teeth.

"Vienna, it's nice to meet you." He paused, attaching the pump's tubing to the raft, then began blowing it up. The soft whoosh of air filling the raft felt reassuring, as if this torture might come to an end eventually. "I'm a law enforcement ranger here at Isle Royale National Park. Hudson Lawrence."

"Isle Royale?" She blinked. Of course, that made sense—why else would there have been an NPS ranger on hand to help her? But how had she gotten this far out into Superior?

"Yep. I take it you weren't planning on boating all the way out here? In the dark?" His tone insinuated something, like he was questioning her decision-making skills.

"No. Those men were after me, and…" She let the words trail away as another shiver took over her body.

"It's okay. You can explain once you're warm." He finished inflating the raft, sealed the valve and removed the pump. After lowering it into the water at the stern of the boat, where it would be easier to climb into, he called softly for her. "Can you walk? Or do you need help?"

"I can do it." *Hopefully.* She forced her aching joints to rise, then wobbled across the slippery deck until she reached the stern. Hudson helped her over the back gunwale, and she clambered ungracefully into the raft.

While she waited, he vanished forward on the boat for a minute, then returned with an armful of supplies and dropped them down into the raft. A pair of hard plastic oars followed. Then he climbed into the raft himself, loosened the line and pushed off into the darkness toward shore.

It wasn't long before they'd grounded on a narrow stretch of rocky beach. Hudson climbed out and offered his hand. "Sorry, but you'll have to get your feet wet again."

She didn't care. It was dry land. She hadn't been able to feel her toes for ages, anyway. He helped her up to the shore and then dragged the raft up, securing its line to a sturdy tree branch. After removing the items he'd stowed in a dry bag, he pulled out a headlamp. Before flicking it on, he paused, and for a moment all she could hear was the constant pattering of rain and the wind in the trees overhead. No sign of a boat engine.

Seeming satisfied, he turned on the light to the lowest setting. Then he scanned their surroundings, revealing rugged, bare rock and evergreens dripping with rain.

"This way," he said finally. "It's raining too hard for a fire unless we find cover, and we want to get away from the shore where they might see the light."

His dark form was barely visible against the darker backdrop of the trees, but she stumbled after him. When she *thunked* her foot into a rock and nearly went down, he reached back and took her hand. "Here, let me help you."

They clambered up a steep section of the slope and then diverted inland. Spiky, wet evergreen branches batted at her hands and face. The walking felt endless, until finally Hudson's light fell on an overhanging slab of rock that provided a small area of shelter. He helped her duck beneath it. She huddled under the flat surface, tucking her arms around her knees and drawing them to her chest.

"I've got to try to find some dry kindling," he said, dropping his supply pack next to her. "Be right back, okay?"

"Here, take this." She held out his hat. He slipped it on, tugging the headlamp lower over his hat, before turning away into the woods. The light from his headlamp flickered between the trees for a few minutes, then vanished.

She hugged her knees tighter. What if he didn't come back? What if those men found her first? An image of Dr. Glickman, face down in a growing pool of blood, filled her mind again, and she knotted her hands into fists. Who were they, and what did they want from her? Was it possible someone outside of BMRL had found out about the new data she'd been ready to show Dr. Glickman? *How?*

Hudson came back long before she had any answers. After ducking back under the overhang, he pulled out an armful of wood from beneath his jacket. "It's not much, but it's all I could find that was reasonably dry. Though dry might be stretching it." He glanced at her, and she squinted in the light from his headlamp. "Sorry." He removed his hat, tugged the lamp off his head and propped it up on a rock, illuminating a patch of ground in front of her. "Can you get that life jacket off by yourself? And the outer coat. It'll help you dry out."

Right, of course. She didn't have to just sit here suffering. Her frozen fingers weren't the most helpful for squeezing the plastic buckles on the life jacket, but after a few minutes she managed it. Then she shrugged off the sopping lab coat. At least her pullover underneath was a synthetic fleece—it'd dry quickly once there was a fire.

Hudson arranged the wood he'd found into a pyramid shape, then filled the center with smaller bits of kindling. When he pulled a container of matches out of his pack and lit the first one, she nearly collapsed with relief.

It took a few tries to get the damp kindling to catch, and even longer to nurture the small flame into a true fire, but eventually there was enough of a crackling blaze that the heat warmed her face, and the smell of smoke filled the air. She stretched her hands close, trying to get enough feeling back to tackle her bootlaces. Her fingers burned with pins and needles as the sensation started to return.

"Need some help with your shoes?" Hudson asked. He crouched down next to her, close enough to help but keeping a respectful distance from her personal space.

"Thanks." She smiled ruefully and stretched her legs toward him. "My fingers are too frozen to untie these knots." In the flickering firelight she could finally get a good look at her rescuer as he set to work on her bootlace. Medium length, light-colored hair—blond she'd guess, rather than gray, because he looked like he couldn't be more than early to mid-thirties at the most. His eyes were a light shade, too, maybe blue or green. No wedding ring graced his nimble fingers, but a few small scars indicated he was used to working with his hands.

And the manner in which he'd handled the boat and the rest of this operation made it seem like he'd been a ranger for a while. He certainly knew his way around Isle Royale.

He tugged her first boot free, and she wrestled off the soggy sock as he worked on the other. Once both feet were bare, she stretched her toes toward the fire, then slipped her pullover off over her head and spread it out on the ground near the heat. Her T-shirt and jeans were still soaked, chilling her back, but there wasn't much she could do about that.

Hudson unzipped his jacket and draped it around her shoulders, then settled onto a rock nearby. "Now, what's going on? Who was chasing you?"

She drew in a deep breath, forcing her mind back to that awful moment in the conference room. "I'm a scientist at a lab in Minnesota, working on a new antibiotic for carbapenem-resistant Enterobacterales and methicillin-resistant *Staphylococcus*—" She stopped as Hudson stiffened, his hands tightening where they rested on his knees. Right, too much scientific jargon. "Sorry, I mean germs that are antibiotic resistant. Anyway, I scheduled a meeting with my supervisor after work to present some really promising lab results, and these men showed up with guns. They stole my laptop and killed my boss—" she swallowed "—and then came for me. The only reason I even made it to the boat is because they apparently need me alive."

His gaze darted to the white lab coat she'd set to one side, then back to the fire without looking at her. When he didn't say anything, she went on. "I was hoping to lose them in some small offshore islands near the lab, but with the wind and the darkness I lost my way. I must've blacked out for a bit because I don't remember anything about the boat flipping until I hit the water."

"It's easy to get disoriented out there, especially in rough conditions." When he looked up from the fire and turned to her, a muscle worked in his jaw, almost like he was clenching his teeth. "What lab do you work for?"

"BioMed Research Lab north of Grand Marais. In Minnesota. Not Michigan."

"Of course, you do," he muttered. One hand tightened into a fist on his knee.

She watched him curiously, waiting for the next question, but he stayed silent, staring into the fire. That muscle feathering in his cheek.

Like he knew more about her situation than he was willing to say.

Hudson forced a slow breath in through his nose and out his mouth. He *needed* to relax, to pretend everything was fine, but how could he? Especially with this fire burning right in front of him, filling his senses with smoke?

The exact same as the night Brittany had died. When he could hear glass exploding inside the building, see the flames licking up the windows, but the authorities wouldn't let him in to find her. That lone scream that he still heard every night just as he was dozing off to sleep, the last sound she'd ever made.

"Ranger Lawrence? Are you all right?" Vienna's soft voice cut through the memories threatening to drown him.

He cleared his throat. "Yeah, of course." Forcing a smile, he added, "You can call me Hudson. I, uh, knew someone who worked for BMRL. Brittany Warners. Maybe you worked with her?"

Warners. Even though they'd married fresh out of undergrad, she'd already had papers published in scientific journals under her maiden name. So officially she'd kept it, but their friends had always known them as Hudson and Brittany Lawrence.

"Oh, yes. I mean, I never met her in person." Vienna watched him as she spoke, like she was trying to puzzle out his reaction. "But we worked together remotely while I was doing my postdoc. She was an excellent chemist and a truly kind person."

A lump formed in his throat. *Great.* He ran a hand over his hair to cover the way he had to blink a few times. She'd been gone just over two years—did he *have* to keep getting this emotional? "Yeah, she was." Time for a redirect, stat. "So, you said the men took your laptop. What do you think they wanted? The data you were presenting? Other research?"

Was that something people killed for? And—the cogs spun in the back of his mind—was there any chance the lab fire that killed his wife *wasn't* an accident? Surely not. That had been a long time ago. Still, the thought bothered him, like a burr stuck in a sock, rubbing against raw skin. He'd never questioned the results of the police investigation after her death. But now, he wasn't so sure. Why did horrible things keep happening at this lab?

"It had to have been the new data." Vienna shrugged. "Though, I have no idea who they are or how they found out about it. For my postdoc research, I developed a genetic algorithm that predicts new formulas for synthetic antibiotics. The team Brittany was part of at BMRL synthesized the most promising ones, which were then tested in tissue culture cells for effectiveness. When I was hired at the lab a year ago, I took over the experiments. As I intended to tell Dr. Glickman tonight, I've found one that works against all the worst superbugs and has no deleterious side effects for the host cells." Her dark eyes burned with an intensity that reminded him of Brittany and how much she'd loved her work. "This antibiotic could change the face of modern medicine."

"Why do they want it? Money? I thought big pharma dropped out of research into antibiotics because it was too expensive."

"It is, and they did. Dr. Glickman founded his lab with the intention of focusing on a higher calling—helping the sick who couldn't find help elsewhere. There are a few other small pharmaceutical companies like ours, struggling to stay afloat. The thing is, with the data I've collected over the last couple of weeks, we'd be almost guaranteed a grant big enough to push the drug through clinicals and on to the market."

Brittany would've been so excited. He swallowed the painful thought. "So…a competing company?"

She chewed her lip. "Maybe. I need to know more. And I need to get back to the lab to download my backup data now that they have my laptop. Unless they found the solid-state drive, too." She turned wide eyes up at him then shook her head. "But they wouldn't be able to access it. Or even the right data on my laptop…" Her voice trailed off, and her throat bobbed.

"Without you…?" he supplied.

She nodded. Pressed her fingers to her mouth. Then, she said softly, "That's why they want me alive. What do I do?"

Pressure built behind his eyes as a wave of exhaustion passed over him. He'd come out here to Isle Royale to leave the world and its problems behind, especially anything having to do with that lab. His fellow forest rangers in Superior National Forest had understood his need to escape Grand Marais and all the memories, and his supervisor had been key in helping him secure one of the rare year-round positions at Isle Royale.

Sure, they worked crazy long hours out here, often in uncomfortable or dangerous conditions, but he loved the challenge. The test of his physical strength and endurance, the opportunity to help visitors stay safe while they explored this corner of God's beautiful creation.

Far away from burning research labs and painful memories. Now here was another woman from the same place, looking up at him with worried eyes, desperate for help.

No. Not every person here needed to be his responsibility. Especially when there were plenty of police officers in Grand Marais.

He smiled reassuringly. "We'll get you safe and sound back to the ranger station at Windigo, and from there, we'll contact the Grand Marais police to report what happened at the lab. They'll get officers there right away and arrange to escort you back. Okay?"

She worried her lower lip but nodded.

"In fact, as soon as this storm passes, we can head back to the boat. That'll be long enough and we should be fine." At least, he *hoped* it would be long enough to lose the men after them. Surely in these conditions, nobody would stay out for long.

But in the back of his mind, the questions lingered. Just who was after Vienna, and how badly did they need her?

Vienna leaned against the rock behind her, letting her eyes drift shut for a minute. The ranger, Hudson, had slipped into a moody silence. Rain continued to pour down outside their protective alcove, punctuated by low rumbles of thunder. Occasionally he'd stoke the fire, causing bigger flames to shoot up from the hot, glowing coals. He'd offered to go search for more wood, but her limbs had thawed out enough that there was no point making him go out in the rain.

She had to admit, the fact he'd known Brittany was unexpected. Weird, even. There had to be more to the story, but he'd given off the very clear impression he didn't want to talk about her. Not that it mattered. As soon as they got back to the ranger station, she'd be able to get in touch with the Cook County Sheriff's Office and make sure her hard drive was secure at the lab. All the data was backed up on the cloud, anyway, and she had her own copy at home. The data would be fine.

When she opened her eyes a short time later, the fire had dwindled to red embers and the rain had stopped. Heavy, damp mist clung to the rock and trees outside their alcove— she couldn't see it in the darkness, but she could smell it. Feel it. Blanketing the world in stillness.

Hudson stood on the other side of the fire, outside their makeshift shelter, his boots and legs barely visible as two black pillars in the darkness. When she shifted, he turned and crouched next to her.

"Rain stopped." He whispered the words, but they still felt jarring in the utter stillness. "You up for heading back to the boat?"

"Sure." The night didn't look exactly welcoming, but the sooner they got back, the sooner she could call the police. She slid her feet back into her socks and boots, which were now only slightly damp. Then she handed Hudson his coat and slipped her pullover back over her head. While Hudson stamped out the remains of the fire, she gathered up the lab coat and life jacket.

The way back felt longer than their initial flight through the rain earlier in the night. She slipped and slid across wet patches of rock, even with her hiking boots. Thank goodness their lab had a casual dress code. Otherwise, she might've been out here in heels. Water dripped from the trees in soft *plunks*, and wet branches dragged across her sleeves and legs. So much for being dry.

The gentle lapping of water on the lakeshore heralded their arrival at the cove. As they reached the edge of the trees, Hudson clicked off his headlamp and paused. "You'd better wait here while I check things out. Just to be safe."

"Okay." She tucked her arms across her chest, hugging the damp life jacket and lab coat. Stars twinkled overhead through the trees, and in the west the moon had re-emerged, leaving a trail of liquid light rippling across the water in the cove.

He moved quietly out from the woods, his boots crunching on gravel as he navigated across the open stretch of shore to where he'd tied up the dinghy. The cove looked safe from here—no sign of life except for their own boat still floating at anchor in the darkness.

Some of the tension ebbed out from her body. Maybe they'd truly lost those men, and this nightmare was almost over. A sigh slipped through her lips.

Then a branch cracked nearby.

She froze. An animal—it had to be an animal. No doubt this place was packed with wildlife.

Her heart shot up into her throat anyway as she debated whether to follow Hudson or keep waiting. Almost subconsciously she edged closer to the nearest tree, its pine needles poking sharp and wet into the exposed skin on her face and hands.

She'd almost made up her mind to leave her hiding place and head for the shore when a wet rag clamped over her mouth, filling her senses with a mildly sweet, pungent odor she'd recognize anywhere after a decade in a lab. Diethyl ether.

Her knees went weak and her head started to swim, even though her heart pounded double time. She clawed at the muscled arm wrapped around her rib cage. Her kicking feet met only air as her captor lifted her.

The last thing she heard was the soft thud of the life jacket and lab coat hitting the ground. Then blackness overtook her.

THREE

The raft was right where Hudson had left it, secured to a tree. He ran the headlamp over it, his fingers obscuring most of the light, just to make sure everything looked intact. A huff of relief escaped his lips as he stowed the survival pack into the front. Out on the water, the patrol boat waited patiently at anchor.

He listened in the darkness for a minute, then released his fingers to let the headlamp shine. No boat engine exploded to life. No gunfire resounded over the still water. Vienna's pursuers must have given up, as he'd hoped.

The knot in his chest loosened. Now all he needed to do was get her safely back to Windigo and into the hands of the Grand Marais authorities. Then she wouldn't be his responsibility anymore. Soft rustling sounded in the trees where she was waiting. Must be growing impatient to get moving.

He didn't want to risk the noise of calling for her. Plus she'd have a hard time covering this uneven terrain in the dark, so he made his way back across the shoreline to where he'd left her.

"Vienna?" he called softly into the stand of fir and spruce trees. "All clear."

No answer. Uneasiness tugged at his gut. Had he misjudged the distance he'd traveled?

Then his headlamp snagged on something on the ground. Her white lab coat, and a short distance away, half-tucked beneath low branches, the neon yellow of the life jacket.

His stomach clenched. In the distance, the low rumble of an engine carried across the water. She'd been here just minutes ago—there was no way they could've swiped her and reached their boat *that* fast.

No, that boat had to be headed for a pickup. And judging by the fact the captors had been this close and left him alone, they weren't looking to tangle with more authorities. The meeting point couldn't be in this cove, but somewhere close by.

Which meant he still had a chance to catch up with them. He clicked off the headlamp and pulled his gun free from its holster, then stood listening for a moment. No telltale light twinkled through the trees—they must be using night vision goggles. Where would a nearby boat landing make the most sense?

Adrenaline demanded that his feet start moving, but instead he stood still, listening.

North. The engine sounded like it was moving north, far out enough on the water he couldn't see it in the faint moonlight. If it was heading for the next cove, the men would have to haul Vienna northwest. They only had a few minutes' head start, and his chances of rescuing her were better on land than by sea.

Leaving the raft and patrol boat behind, he climbed up the rocky wall at the north end of the beach. If he could get close enough to them, maybe he'd be able to hear them. Every step felt too loud on the rocky ground as gravel crunched and twigs snapped beneath his boots. Though he wanted to run, he forced himself to slow his pace, to pause every few steps to listen. The sound of the engine vanished once he left the open shoreline and entered the forest, and the little bit of moonlight guiding his steps disappeared into shadow. A lone bird took up its early-morning song somewhere nearby.

Unlike whoever had taken Vienna, he didn't have night vision goggles. He'd have to risk using the headlamp to illuminate his path. He held it low and covered it with a corner of his shirt. At least that would help diminish its glaring brightness.

He'd spent probably ten minutes working his way through the woods, his pace painfully slow, when a low murmuring sound reached his ears. What was that? Voices? Holding his breath, he listened for a moment and pressed the headlamp into his stomach to cut its light.

Yes, those were definitely voices. He couldn't make out the words, but it sounded like two men, and not far ahead. Slowly he felt his way forward, inching over the rocky ground between the trees.

"That way," a low voice insisted. "Fuller said a quarter click, bearing 272."

"Well, he didn't have to carry her through all these blasted trees," came the reply. "Here, you take a turn."

One of them grunted, like he was hoisting a heavy weight. They must've knocked Vienna out somehow. This was probably the best chance Hudson was going to get. He had to find some way to intervene without hurting her. At least he had the element of surprise—*if* he could reach them undetected.

A distraction would help. Keeping his headlamp dark, he brushed his fingers along the ground until he found a decent, baseball-size rock. Then he lobbed it toward the west, as if he'd been following their original trail.

"What was that?" one of the men whispered.

"Has to be the ranger." The other man made a noise that sounded almost like a growl. "We shoulda killed him."

Anger fired through Hudson's blood, but he had to keep his movements precise. And take advantage of their distraction. Easing the headlamp away from his stomach, he let a little of its light trickle through his shirt fabric to illuminate the path. Then he edged forward, taking each step as quietly as he could.

"That would've been stupid," the other man replied, "and you know it. The boss doesn't want anyone to know we were out here."

His voice was close now, really close. Like on the other side of these branches. Hudson took one steadying breath, then tossed his headlamp out between them.

"What the—" Two sets of night vision goggles swiveled toward the light. Vienna hung limply over one of their shoulders, a rag tied over her mouth and nose.

Hudson lunged at the other man, who grunted in surprise as they crashed to the ground. "Go!" the man yelled to his companion while attempting to flip Hudson over onto his back. But Hudson had his gun ready and brought the handle down hard onto the side of the man's head. The man groaned and went limp.

He spared a few seconds to secure the man's hands with zip ties from his utility belt before climbing to his feet. The one carrying Vienna had vanished through the trees heading west, but his crashing footsteps were so loud he'd be easy to follow.

Hudson snatched up the headlamp off the ground and kept the light on the path in front of him as he raced after the other man. With his speed advantage, it only took a minute before he'd caught up.

"Freeze!" he yelled.

The man ignored him and fired a gun over his shoulder, the sharp cracks splitting through the night air. Hudson lunged behind the cover of a tree, but the shots went wide. He couldn't risk firing back, not with Vienna in the way.

Instead, he holstered his gun and dashed sideways into the woods, plowing ahead, heedless of the branches whipping into his face and arms, until he'd drawn parallel with the man. Then he angled over, cutting between the trees, and tackled the man to the ground.

They landed hard, Vienna sandwiched between them. His headlamp went flying, but its bright glow illuminated the small space between the trees. Hudson ripped the gag off her mouth and shoved her out of the way, more roughly than he would've liked, but keeping her alive was the priority.

His opponent used the opportunity to punch Hudson in the cheek, whipping his head sideways. He ignored the stinging of the blow and landed one of his own. The other man brought his gun up, but Hudson struck it away. They rolled across the ground, wrestling for control, until the man managed to pin him and wrap his hands around Hudson's throat.

Something sharp dug into his side, and while he tried to fend off the man's grip with one hand, his other fingers scrabbled against the dirt until they wrapped around a small rock. He snatched it up and brought it down hard on the back of the other man's head with a sharp *thwack*. The man groaned and went limp, collapsing on top of Hudson.

He rolled his opponent off to one side and scrambled to his feet, brushing debris off his clothing. Vienna still lay where he'd left her, but she was stirring now. She slowly sat up and blinked as she looked around, a dazed expression on her face.

She frowned up at him. "What…happened?"

"They found you." He pointed to the rag as he picked up the headlamp. "Must've knocked you out somehow."

She nodded. "Diethyl ether. Would've been more Nancy Drew if they used chloroform, but maybe they heard that takes longer."

He held out a hand. "Can you stand? They were taking you to meet their boat. It's only a matter of time before someone suspects things didn't go as planned."

She slid her hand into his, and he pulled her to her feet. When she wobbled, he braced an arm around her back.

"I'm okay," she insisted, shaking her head like she was clearing off cobwebs. "Which way?"

Shining his headlamp on the path ahead, he led her back toward the cove where they'd left the patrol boat. The men must've seen it and then decided to wait for him and Vienna to return, rather than searching for them farther inland.

The chatter of the birds had grown over the last few minutes, and by the time they reached the raft, the darkness in the east was lightening to a milky twilight. He couldn't hear the other boat engine, but he had no doubt as soon as he fired up his patrol boat, they'd notice.

Working quickly, he untied the raft and helped Vienna inside, then pushed off and rowed out to the patrol boat. Vienna climbed in first, and he handed the oars and survival pack to her. After he climbed aboard, he hauled the raft up and opened the quick-release valve. Putting it away would have to come later.

"Just stow those wherever you find a good place." He pointed at the gear Vienna had unloaded. "I'll get the anchor up before we start the engine, just in case they hear it."

He crawled out to the bow and worked the anchor free. After pulling it up and stowing it in place, he returned to the console and flipped on the depth sounder. Vienna was attempting to refold the wet raft, but he waved her off. "Don't worry about that yet. Just tuck it under the seats."

She shoved the partially rolled raft beneath one of the seats and joined him at the console, holding on to the frame as he started the engine, put it in gear and eased the boat around.

"As soon as they hear us, they're likely to chase. Probably even fire at us." He searched her face in the dim light. Weariness tugged at her features, and dark circles had gathered beneath her brown eyes.

But she showed no sign of fear, only of resolve. "How can I help?"

"Keep an eye on the depth sounder for me. I know these waters well, but if things get hairy, you might need to drive." He patted the firearm at his side, and she nodded, her throat bobbing.

They headed out of the cove and into the waters of Lake Superior, still choppy after the previous night's storm but nowhere near as rough. The patrol boat flew over the waves as he pushed the engine faster, heading southwest around a headland and into North Gap, then turning south. They passed over the 1928 wreck of the *SS America* and sped toward Washington Harbor heading east.

He glanced over his shoulder, checking for signs of the other boat as the sky grew lighter and the stars vanished overhead. Was that the faint sound of another engine? His gaze met Vienna's, her eyes wide. She'd heard it, too.

This time when he looked back, the other boat's light flashed in the distance as it rounded the headland after them.

Only four miles to go. But could they make it?

Vienna clutched the metal bar until her knuckles hurt. She pressed her other hand against her chest. Exhaustion mingled with lingering dizziness from the ether, threatening to collapse her knees. *Sorry, body, now's not the right time.*

She gritted her teeth and tore her gaze away from the light chasing them down. Hudson cranked up the engine's speed, zooming toward the empty harbor faster than was probably allowed. He freed one hand from the wheel and made a call on a built-in radio, notifying an invisible listener about the chase and requesting backup. Hopefully whoever was on the other end had the power to make things happen. Fast.

Despite their speed, the boat behind them was creeping closer with each passing minute. Loud cracks of gunfire echoed across the water, but the shots fell short. Hudson glanced over his shoulder, then to her, like he was considering whether he needed to hand off the wheel and fire back.

Please, no. She wasn't a bad pilot, despite what had happened last night, but after that experience… Her heart raced at the mere thought of taking the wheel.

But he faced forward again and said, "Hold on. They don't know these waters as well as I do. We might be able to run them aground."

Not a bad plan, especially since the other boat appeared larger. The patrol boat would have an advantage with its shallower draft.

He swerved the boat to the left, then banked back to the right, bringing it in close enough to shore that the rocky cliff and tree line towered above their heads. She swayed on her feet, clinging tighter to the metal bar. Wind whipped her disheveled hair into her face and mouth. Behind them, the other boat followed, firing off more shots. Bullets pinged off the cliff wall nearby, sending a spray of rocks into the water in the boat's wake.

"They're getting closer!" she yelled, brushing hair away from her face.

"We're almost to the harbor," he called back. "There's Beaver Island."

That dark mass ahead of them? It was a good thing he knew where he was going, because she could hardly see a thing.

With another round of sharp cracks, gunfire rang across the water, close enough to send spray across their backs. Hudson's shoulders were rigid as he veered the boat back and forth into a nauseating zigzag, drawing them closer to the island with each pass. The other boat bore down on them.

The patrol boat headed straight for the island, as if he were going to run them aground right onto a promontory. At the last second, he veered to the right, cutting a wide swath around a long, dark dock jutting out into the water. Behind them, the other pilot narrowly avoided a collision, swerving at the last second and losing distance.

"Look!" Vienna pointed ahead, where a pair of twin lights reflected across the dark water.

Hudson's radio crackled at the same moment. "Patrol boat *Elizabeth Kemmer*, this is the *Minong* en route to help."

"Thank You, Jesus," she prayed aloud, almost at the same moment as he muttered, "Praise the Lord."

They exchanged a glance over the wheel, a brief spark of recognition that they shared the same faith, and then the moment broke as he picked up the radio to reply.

"Copy, *Minong*. Many thanks."

"Get into the dock. We'll handle this," the other ranger replied.

Hudson offered a salute as his patrol boat flew past the other. At the sight of the approaching boat, their pursuers turned sharply to the right, kicking up a giant spray of water.

"They're turning around!" Vienna clutched a hand to

her chest, relief coursing through her insides. Soon both their pursuers and the other ranger boat vanished from view around the other side of the island. Up ahead, a rocky shoreline came into view, dotted with low-lying brown buildings sandwiched between evergreens.

Hudson slowed the boat's speed to reduce its wake and steered around a small point into a protected harbor. A half dozen wooden docks jutted out into the water, with a handful of small boats tied up. He guided the boat up to one of the docks, idled the engine and hopped lightly out onto the dock with a bow line. While he tied it off, she climbed into the stern and found another line, handing it to him. With the boat secure, he cut the engine.

In the east, the first rays of sunlight crested the horizon, creating a hazy orange glow over the nearby rooftops and trees. A full night had passed. Had anyone from the janitorial staff found Dr. Glickman's body yet and reported it to the police? The thought of him lying there, face down on the conference table... She shuddered.

"You all right?" Hudson asked as he gathered a few items from a storage locker.

"I'm okay," she said, stuffing aside the horrible memories. She'd have to relive it all soon enough when she talked to the cops. Lingering nausea from the ether and this awful boat ride weren't helping the situation.

One of his eyes narrowed a fraction, as if he were tempted to press, but instead he offered her a hand and helped her out of the boat. "Let's get you back to the ranger station."

The walk wasn't far, and the rich scent of damp earth and pine felt like a balm to her soul. As familiar here on this side of the lake as it was at home, or back during her carefree childhood in Maine. She'd never been able to get

Jack to understand why she loved the woods so much. He'd been more of the watch-nature-documentaries-on-TV rather than the go-out-and-explore type.

When they reached the small ranger station and visitor center, Hudson unlocked the door and flipped on the lights. "They won't be opening to the public for a few more hours," he explained. The interior was beautiful—golden pine on the floor, the walls and the ceiling. The dark knots and wood grain made her feel like she'd entered a log cabin. He led the way past wildlife displays, around a counter and to a door at the back. Behind it, a smaller room contained a bookcase, filing cabinets, a counter with a small sink and an assortment of desks squashed against the walls, taking up the floor space. But there wasn't any wind or rain, and when Hudson offered her a padded rolling chair, she slumped into it gratefully.

In a matter of minutes, he'd brewed her up a cup of coffee and was punching in the Cook County Sheriff Office's number onto the phone on one of the desks. He punched the button for speakerphone and sat on the edge of the desk, listening as it rang. After the dispatcher answered, Hudson identified himself and gave a brief explanation about Vienna, then waited as she transferred the call.

"This is Chief Deputy Nielson," a male voice responded after the dispatcher identified Hudson and Vienna. His tone sounded gravelly, like he'd been awake for hours and coffee wasn't quite doing the trick. "Ranger Lawrence, take us off speakerphone please."

Something about his tone made Vienna shift uncomfortably in her seat. What was going on? Hudson picked up the phone and jabbed a button on the machine.

His eyebrows quirked as his gaze landed on her. "About

five foot six, brown hair, brown eyes. She told me her name."

A swarm of bees buzzed through her stomach. Why was there even a question that she might be lying?

Some of the worry settled down as he detailed what they'd gone through the previous night, how her boat had flipped and he'd rescued her. How the other boat had chased them, fired at them, found them again that morning. She leaned back in her seat, suddenly exhausted. Somehow, she'd have to come up with the energy to explain what had happened at the lab, too.

"No, I had no opportunity to attempt identifying them." Hudson slid off the desk and stood, leaning against it with one hand while he pressed the phone to his ear with the other. His gaze went to a clock over the door. "A patrol boat was chasing. I haven't received an update."

He grew quiet and listened for a few minutes, his brow crinkling. When he glanced at her again, something had shifted in his expression. Like he was working on a math problem and the figures weren't adding up. "Okay, will do. Thanks, Chief Deputy Nielson. We'll be in touch."

Hudson placed the handset back on the receiver and stared at it for a long moment, then turned to her, his blue eyes hard as glittering gemstones. She held her breath, resisting the urge to shrink in on herself.

He surveyed her for a long moment in tense silence, but then his expression softened. A long breath escaped his lips. "The sheriff's office has a warrant out for your arrest. Vienna, you're the main suspect in the destruction of BMRL property and the killing of Dr. Kevin Glickman."

FOUR

"What?" Vienna's stomach dropped. Hot coffee sloshed out of her mug, searing her skin, but she barely noticed as she set it on the desk. How could the police think it was *her*?

Hudson dragged a hand through his hair. "A janitor found Dr. Glickman's body and called the police around three a.m. There was no evidence of forced entry. Whoever entered the building had an access card."

"No." She shook her head vehemently. "There were at least three of them. More than that, because they were talking on comms. They had to have broken in." The building's doors locked automatically every time they were closed. More than once she or a colleague had locked themselves out accidentally going to lunch without their key card. "And what about the outdoor security cameras?"

"Malfunctioned. The footage is all black. The police think someone tampered with the cameras."

For once she wished Dr. Glickman had installed interior cameras. But he'd always trusted his employees and wanted to encourage a collaborative work environment where people didn't feel watched.

"There wasn't anything missing," he went on. "At least nothing obvious. They won't know about data breaches on the lab computers until they can let the employees in to check."

Please, God, not my data. Although even as she silently tossed the prayer up to Heaven, she had no doubt what those men had wanted. What they'd been willing to kill for. "Why do they think it was *me*?" she asked.

"More than one witness testified that you hadn't left yet when they did yesterday, and Dr. Glickman's wife said he'd told her he was staying late for a meeting with you."

She closed her eyes. Unfortunately, that all made sense. Her boss wouldn't have any reason to keep their meeting secret from Melissa. When she reopened her eyes, Hudson was staring at her intently. "But staying late doesn't make me a killer."

"It's not just that." A crease sliced between his brows. "The murder weapon was outside, tossed in a bush not far from the dock where you took Dr. Glickman's boat, and your access card and cell phone were found on the floor near the body."

"I left everything at the lab when I ran!" She lifted her hands, shaking them as she spoke. How could this not be obvious? "They must've found my workspace and taken my things." Which meant…

She stared down at his desk, tracing the lines of wood grain without really seeing anything. Her hands dropped, and the anger of a second before fizzled like a fire doused with cold water. If they'd found her lab, surely they'd taken the computer tower, too. And the external hard drive. If it had been *her* stealing that data, she'd have grabbed anything not bolted down. And if it was all gone, the only backup she had left was at her home.

Unless they'd found that, too? A knot tighter than a cinched bowline wrapped around her chest.

"The police in Grand Marais will have to sort that out." Hudson's words snapped her attention back to the immediate problem.

She looked up at him again, startled to see something silver flash in his hands. Metal clinked as he flipped open a pair of handcuffs.

"Vienna Clayton, I'm placing you under arrest. You have the right to remain silent—"

She blinked at him as he rattled off her Miranda rights, her brain suddenly too sluggish to understand how everything was happening so fast. When he stared down at her hands, she held them up like an obedient child. Cold metal brushed her skin, raising goose bumps, as he snapped the cuffs into place.

"What are you going to do with me?" she asked. The question came out in small puffs, like she couldn't find enough air. "And my data. If they get into my house and take it, there'll be no—"

A radio on his belt beeped. He picked it up and answered, exchanging a brief, staticky call with another ranger. She could only make out a few words, like *boat* and *away*.

Hudson's frown confirmed her suspicions a minute later when he signed off. "The boat that was chasing us fled the scene. They weren't able to identify who was driving it."

She held up her cuffed hands. "Shouldn't that be all the evidence you need I'm not involved in this? *You* were with me last night. You saw what happened."

"Look, I'll be happy to testify to everything I witnessed, but this isn't my case." He dragged a hand through his hair, then reached for the phone. "In fact, I need to call Chief Deputy Nielson back and let him know you're in custody. They'll send a boat over to pick you up."

How long would that take? And then how much longer

before she could convince them to let her go? By then the data backup at her house would be long gone, if those men hadn't found it already.

"Wait." She leaned forward, reaching for his arm with her cuffed hands. In a flash, he dropped the phone receiver and grabbed her wrists with a grip so strong it caught her off guard.

Warning flared in his eyes, but then his expression softened. Maybe from the startled look plastered across her face. "You're not going to cause trouble, are you?" he asked. The tone was gentle, but there was an undercurrent of steel. This man wasn't someone she'd want to face as a true adversary.

"No," she said meekly. "I just want to say something before you call them."

"Very well." He released her, leaning back and crossing his arms over his chest. Her skin felt suddenly cold where his hands had been. "Go ahead."

"You know how I told you about my data? The formula they're trying to steal?"

He nodded.

"They have my laptop, and if they found my phone and access card, that means they must've gotten into my lab, too. But I have one more backup of the data at my home. If they didn't get to it yet, there's still a chance I could save it."

He reached for the phone again. "Great, let's tell the pol—"

"No." This time instead of grabbing for him, she held up her hands above her lap. "I need to get it. I can't risk handing off instructions and them not listening, or taking so long that those men get there first. If they didn't already." Years' worth of work, and not just for her, but for all her coworkers. And it could all be gone. The thought choked the air in her lungs, and she pressed her hands to her chest.

"It's going to be fine," he said. "Calm down. The police can handle it."

"You don't understand." Tears sprang into the corners of her eyes, and she blinked, sucking in a deep breath. "Dr. Glickman just died because of this discovery. *I* nearly died. And all the other people who've worked on this project— they've dedicated years to making this breakthrough." As she spoke, his expression shifted, softening again. Like maybe a tiny part of him was listening. She had one last card to play. "You said you knew someone who worked with me—Brittany Warners. We would never have figured out the right formula without her. You'd be honoring her memory, too, if you help me make sure that data stays safe."

She'd made her plea. Now all she could do was pray that this man she'd just met, her only chance for help, would listen.

Hudson's insides churned worse than last night's storm-tossed waves on the lake. Every mention of Brittany opened up a deep and painful wound, one that would never heal. Might as well be one of Vienna's antibiotic-resistant infections in his heart.

"What are you asking me to do?" he ground out. Because the last thing he wanted was to get any more involved than he already was. He wanted to sit here in this comfortable office, drinking coffee and twiddling his thumbs until a Cook County deputy turned up and escorted Ms. Clayton away. Sure, he'd tell them all about what happened last night, but that was supposed to be it. End of story.

Instead, as Vienna kept talking, all he could think was that this was God's twisted sense of humor. *Here, Hudson, let me take your wife away and then send you a brutal reminder of your loss just when you thought you were moving on with your life.*

"I want *you* to take me to the police." Vienna pinned him with her dark brown gaze. "Tell them you're bringing me over, and on the way, we make our own extra stop at my house. It's just north of the city, right on the lake. It'll only take a few minutes for me to run in and grab the external hard drive, and then we can be back on our way to the police department. You'll never have to see me again."

He absorbed her words slowly, turning them over in his mind. That chief deputy over in Grand Marais would probably thank him for saving one of his officers a trip across the lake. And they had enough rangers to cover his duties here for half a day. It would be easier to let the police handle all of it, but if what Vienna said was true—and he had no reason to doubt her—then Brittany's work was in danger, too. She would have been just as panicky as Vienna was at the thought of losing what they'd gained.

Then there was all of last night lingering in the back of his mind. What if those men were still chasing Vienna? After what they'd experienced last night, he didn't believe for one minute that she was actually guilty of vandalism, murder or theft. He'd heard the men talking and seen their tactics. No doubt they'd tried to frame her to cover up their tracks.

He had full faith the police would reach the same conclusion. But would it take them too long? Would Vienna's formula be compromised before then?

His jaw ached, and he realized he was clenching his teeth. If there was one thing he'd learned about God, it was that God was infinite and he wasn't. Hudson would never understand why God operated the way He did. Why

He chose to let certain things happen. Why this woman, who'd known his wife, was now begging him for help. How could he say no?

Lord, I hope You know what You're doing. Because Hudson sure didn't.

"Fine, we'll stop on the way," he ground out, reaching for the phone. The look of gratitude and relief that washed over her face *almost* made it worth it. He'd spent so long hiding over here on Isle Royale, it'd been a long time since he'd been in a position to make a difference in someone's life on a personal level.

Chief Deputy Nielson picked up after the call was patched through to his office. When Hudson made his offer to bring her over himself, the other man hesitated. "She's wanted for murder, Ranger Lawrence. You sure you have enough support?"

He glanced sideways at Vienna. She was playing with the long ends of her hair, running her fingers along the strands. The woman hardly looked like murderer material. Obviously the police had yet to hear her version of the story. Maybe it would take them longer to untangle everything than he'd thought.

"I'll be fine," he said gruffly. "She's cooperating."

After ending the call, he updated the chief ranger on his plan. Vienna sat quietly, cuffed hands in her lap, as he rushed his way through a brief explanation and promised a detailed report of the night's events later. By the time his boss had given him approval and he'd hung up the phone, it felt like an entire day had already passed. Yet the clock only read 7:37 a.m. The ranger working the desk in here wouldn't even arrive for another ten minutes or so.

"I need coffee," he stated. "You want a refill?"

"No, thank you. I'm fine."

He could feel her eyes on him as he picked up the carafe and poured the steaming black liquid into a mug. No K-Cups or disposable paper here. And also no time to waste. He took a few sips, letting the hot liquid fortify his spirits for the day ahead.

"Black?" Vienna asked. Her nose crinkled, and he couldn't help chuckling at her expression.

"Cream and sugar water down the caffeine." He took a few more swigs, then dumped the contents in the sink and left the mug on his desk next to the one she'd used. Washing dishes could wait. "All right, let's get out of here before visitors start showing up."

Color flared in her cheeks as she glanced at the cuffs.

"Sorry," he offered, "but I have to leave them on you at least until we get onto the boat. Rules are rules."

He took her by the arm and guided her out of the room, flipping off the lights behind them. As they were leaving the visitor center, another ranger came striding up the path. Hudson touched the brim of his hat in salute as he and Vienna moved to one side.

"Lawrence," the other ranger acknowledged. His gaze snagged on Vienna, then drifted down to the flash of silver at her wrists. His brow furrowed as he glanced back to Hudson.

"Morning, Henrick. I'll explain later," he replied. "You working the desk?"

The other man nodded, then took the door Hudson was holding open. He and Vienna resumed their march down to the dock, where the *Elizabeth Kemmer* still rocked gently. After helping Vienna board, he took a few minutes to examine the vessel for damage after the previous night's gunfire. Other than a few nicks and dings, the boat appeared to be in working order.

"Looks good," he announced to Vienna. She sat on the bench seat behind the console, knuckles nearly white where she clutched a metal bar. He climbed aboard and walked over to her. "Hey, you okay?"

She nodded, blinking rapidly. "Sorry. I'm just tired. And it's…" She swallowed. "It's hard getting back on a boat after last night."

"You have every reason to feel that way." He reached out to touch her shoulder but stopped himself. What was he thinking? They'd only just met. "But with the storm over and your pursuers long gone, we're going to be fine."

As if to help his argument, a boat engine hummed gently in the distance, and a moment later the *Minong* curved gracefully into the harbor. He waited as the other boat pulled up alongside the dock. Caroline, an older woman who'd served more summers than he could count on the island, tossed him a rope to tie off at the bow then cut the engine. The other ranger, a newbie fresh out of the Park Ranger Law Enforcement Academy whose name Hudson couldn't remember, sprang over the gunwale and secured the stern like it was his biggest goal in life.

Hudson glanced between them. "What happened?"

"They took off as soon as we appeared," Caroline said. "Back across the lake heading west-northwest. Jonas tried to ID them but…" She shook her head.

Jonas—that was his name. Enough seasonal rangers came and went it was hard to keep track sometimes. But the kid had enthusiasm, Hudson had to give him credit for that.

"Sorry, Ranger Lawrence, sir." Jonas stood from where he'd just knotted off the line and brushed off his hands. "The boat didn't have any distinctive markings, and the people aboard were all dressed in black."

As he'd witnessed firsthand. He clapped the younger man on the shoulder. "Thanks for trying."

"We didn't see any sign of the boat that sank, but the recovery team will start the search for it soon. You heading back out already?" Caroline nodded toward the *Elizabeth Kemmer*, where Vienna waited. She'd dropped her hands into her lap, hiding the cuffs, though the other two probably couldn't see her under the shadow of the canopy. A twinge of pity passed through his system—that had to be embarrassing, on top of all the other emotional and physical pain she'd endured in the past eighteen hours. He hoped the police would be able to clear her name quickly.

"Yeah, I'm escorting Ms. Clayton back to Grand Marais." He left out the part about her being a suspect in a murder case. The other two would find out soon enough once word spread through the ranks.

Caroline saluted. "Safe travels."

She and Jonas headed up the dock, their thumping footsteps echoing over the soft sound of water lapping against the pilings. Hudson climbed aboard his boat and started the engine, then turned to Vienna. "You just sit tight, and we'll be across the lake before you know it."

Dark strands of hair hung around her pale face, and something in her glistening eyes unexpectedly twisted his heart. He had the sudden, compelling urge to sit down next to her, wrap an arm around her shoulders and tell her everything would be all right. To make that fear and confusion go away. The way her lips pressed together as she nodded made it even worse.

But obviously comforting her was out of the question, so instead he forced himself to untie the ropes securing the boat to the dock. The best way to help her now was to get her back to Grand Marais.

"Can you at least remove the cuffs now?" she asked. Her ragged tone didn't help matters.

He dug the keys out of his pocket and knelt in front of her. "Promise not to cause mischief?"

A weary smile tugged at her lips. "You have my word."

She held out her wrists, and he managed to finagle the key into the lock and pop the cuffs free without touching her.

They cast off, and he guided the vessel out of the harbor toward the open waters of Lake Superior. The morning breeze felt fresh and sweet after the oppressive rain of the night before, almost like an unspoken promise that things were going to work out. Sunshine sparkled on the tops of the gently rippling waves, and the open water called to him.

All he needed to do was get Vienna across the lake, let her have her five minutes to grab her data backup, and then deliver her into the hands of the police. They'd be able to unravel this mess to clear her name and find the true culprit.

And then he'd never have to hear about her or her laboratory ever again.

FIVE

The ride across the lake passed in a haze of exhaustion. Vienna kept nodding off, then jolting awake as they hit a wave or the boat made a course correction. Thankfully there was no sign of her pursuers from the night before—that was a small mercy.

But even though Hudson seemed to believe her about what had happened—enough to let her stop at her house—the steely resolve in his eyes could only mean one thing. He was going to turn her in. She was sure of it. All she could do was hope that the police would believe her, too. *God, please help me clear all of this up*, she prayed silently.

Hopefully He was listening. Hopefully He would answer her prayer the way she needed Him to. It made no sense to her why He would allow her to find this formula that could help so many, and then let it be stripped away through evil and injustice. There was no guarantee that men who resorted to theft and murder would ever make this drug easily available to those who needed it. Surely, that couldn't be His will.

Of course, what had happened with Jack and her marriage made no sense, either. Why had God allowed her to marry a man who would later betray her? What was the purpose behind all that suffering?

And Dr. Glickman? Why did he have to lose his life when he had dedicated everything to a noble pursuit?

The questions churned inside, but no answers came as the hours passed. Finally the shoreline came into view as a distant purple haze, and she pulled herself out of her disquieting thoughts as Hudson reduced their speed.

"Where are we?" she asked. Her voice creaked like a rusty hinge after the hours of silence.

He studied his onboard navigation chart for a moment, then turned to her. "A few nautical miles west of your lab. Should be right—" he pointed "—there."

She squinted in the direction he indicated. Sunlight glinted off glass far in the distance, and small buildings appeared as darker blobs against the shore farther south in Grand Marais. It *was* her lab, and he'd clearly been in this area before. "You know these waters."

He stared across the lake as the boat rocked gently in the waves. Almost as if lost in thought. Where had he lived before coming to Isle Royale? What history made those shoulders so rigid as he studied the coastline?

She shook her head at herself. None of that mattered. After he dropped her off at the police department, she'd never see him again. And that was good, because all she needed in life was God and her work. Not another man to leave her.

"My house is in an inlet to the northeast, about ten miles up the coast from the lab."

His eyebrows raised. "Ten miles? That's practically Grand Portage. You told me it was close."

"It *is* close. Fifteen minutes by car, twenty by boat. I'll be boating to work all the time once I save up enough for my own." The words came out more fiercely than she'd intended. Maybe because after Jack had cheated on her and left her and crushed all her hopes to smithereens, she had nothing left but her own dreams. And buying her own boat was one of them.

Hudson held up his hands. "Whoa, there. It's fine. We'll make it work."

"Sorry," she mumbled. "It's… Never mind."

His lips curved down into a half frown, and he almost looked like he was going to ask, but then he turned back to the wheel. "I'll take us northeast along the coast, and you let me know when we're getting close, okay?"

"Sure." She fidgeted with her sleeves, tugging them lower over her wrists. Not much sounded better than a hot shower and sleep, but first she had to get through the hours that lay ahead. Tension knotted up beneath her ribs with each passing minute as the coastline grew larger and they turned to race along it.

Sunshine flashed off cars' windshields on the coastal highway. Any one of them could be fleeing her house with her external hard drive. Or what if that boat was still out here, lurking in a cove and waiting for her?

She shivered. Hopefully the rangers were right, and their pursuers had given up. They had her laptop and probably everything from her lab—they'd find some way to access it without her. Or maybe they'd give up entirely, rather than continue risking run-ins with the law.

That logic rang hollow, but she clung to it, anyway, as she rose on shaky legs to stand next to Hudson and directed him to the little inlet where her small home sat nestled among the pine trees and rocks. The previous owner had gotten too old to maintain the place, and by the time his family had forced him out and decided to sell, they'd practically given the home away. She knew it had been a God thing—she'd been looking to buy at just the right time, and as soon as she'd seen the pictures online from Maryland, she'd snapped the place up without ever visiting in person. It had been a little balm for her soul on the heels of her divorce.

"No sign of other boats," he said, scanning the coastline in both directions.

The huge ball of yarn beneath her ribs untangled a fraction. "It's that one," she said, pointing to her short stretch of dock. He pulled up next to the pilings, and she jumped out to secure the boat. The wood creaked loudly beneath her feet, and she was painfully aware of the slimy buildup of algae on the pilings. When Hudson's gaze caught on hers, she said, "The place wasn't in very good shape when I bought it. The last owner was eighty-five. I'm pretty sure he never came down here."

Hudson stared at the rocky path leading away from the dock, his gaze lingering where it vanished into the trees, before scanning the woods above. One dark corner of her roof jutted through thick evergreen arms, and the lines of the deck were visible as a lighter brown against the dark trunks. It wasn't much—yet—but one day it would be. The two-story was a little unkempt, but it was beautiful. A perfect lakeside home, with its big main level wraparound deck and lower level walkout basement.

"It's gorgeous," he said simply. "Though you'd have a better view if you took down some of those trees."

"I know." It was just a lot to manage. Memories flashed into her mind of Jack, back during their short months of marriage, and how he'd taken care of things like swapping out light bulbs and clearing clogged drains. He'd never been much of a handyman, but at least she hadn't had to do it all alone. She bit her lip before she said something foolish and instead started up the rugged path.

The chattering of birds and the soft earthy smell of the woods soothed her as they trudged ahead. At the top, the path popped them out practically on the patio beneath her deck. Heat crept up her neck as she realized how overgrown it all must look. Maybe in the summer, after everything had settled down, she'd find the time to hire somebody to come clear out some of these scrappy bushes and trees.

Hudson placed a hand on her arm, gentle but firm. "Stop a minute," he whispered, "and let me check things out."

Did he think someone was here? "Okay." The word stuck in her throat like a lump of too-dry baked potato. She pointed to the left. "The driveway is on this side."

He stood listening for a long moment and then cautiously moved out from the cover of the trees, scanning the area as he went. She followed after him, grateful that she wasn't alone. From what they could see of the house, the windows were all intact and the rear sliding doors were still closed on both levels. In the front, her driveway sat empty—her vehicle was still at BMRL, unless the police had impounded it as evidence.

She relaxed a little by the time they reached the front walk and had seen nothing amiss. Her keys were still at the lab, too, or lost somewhere, but she punched in the code for the garage and led Hudson in through the side door, which she kept unlocked unless it was night. A waft of stale, rotting food hit her nose as soon as she pulled the door open. Yuck.

"Sorry for the smell." She winced as she led the way through the laundry-slash-mudroom, where a mound of clothes lay heaped on top of the dryer, waiting to be folded. A short hallway took them past the half bath—a hasty glance as she passed revealed nothing embarrassing—and into the combined open kitchen and living room. Fruit flies buzzed around an apple core on the cutting board and over her sink, and she chided herself for not taking an extra three minutes yesterday to clean up after breakfast. But she'd been in such a rush to get to work and prepare her presentation for Dr. Glickman, she'd scarcely even noticed the mess.

Was this why Jack had left her? Because she was too focused on other things to be a good housekeeper? The thought burned along with her cheeks as she practically dove for the cutting board. Jack had been focused, too, when they'd met—a molecular biology PhD candidate doing his own research. Before he'd decided he wanted something different. She swept the decaying fruit into the trash and set the cutting board in the sink with more force than she'd intended.

"Hey. Vienna." Hudson's gentle tone stopped her short. A smile played on his lips. "Let me take care of that while you get your data."

Right. He was supposed to be escorting her to the police department, not hanging out at her home while she cleaned. She couldn't meet his gaze and beat a hasty retreat out of the kitchen. "Thanks," she mumbled. "The soap and everything is right there."

Obviously. Maybe it was better to stop talking entirely. But Hudson was the first "guest"—not that he was actually a guest—she'd had over to her house. And when she stole a glance back at him, with dish suds working their way up his muscular forearms and a shadow of blond stubble creeping across his strong jaw, there was no denying he was the most attractive man she'd been around in a long time. Since her cheating ex-husband, actually.

Focus, Vienna. He'd made it clear his only goal was to get her to the cops, and that was perfectly fine. She didn't look back again as she crossed the living room and walked to her desk against the opposite wall. To the right, a bank of windows overlooked the offending trees blocking her view of the lake. If you leaned back and forth just so, you could catch a glimpse of blue flashing between the thick branches.

Like the rest of her home, there was no indication her desktop computer had been tampered with. Her breath slipped out between her teeth as relief eased into her chest. The files were still here. It wasn't everything, not like she had at the lab, but all the important stuff was here. She dug a flash drive out of a drawer and initiated a transfer.

A red light flashed on her answering machine—someone had left a message. The landline was a relic leftover from the last homeowner. Now, with her cell phone gone, she was glad she'd kept it. She hit play while she waited for the data transfer.

"Vienna, it's Melissa."

She froze. *Dr. Glickman's wife.* In the kitchen behind her, the sound of clinking dishes died as Hudson grew quiet.

"Honey, I don't know where you are or what happened, but I know you're innocent. I left a message on your cell, too. Call me. Please. I want to help."

Vienna pressed cold hands to her mouth. Poor Melissa— losing her husband, and now this drama with *her.* The older woman had been so generous with her time and advice since Vienna first moved here last year, though a bit more reserved and distant than her husband. Her concern now was so thoughtful. She snatched up the receiver and tapped in Melissa's number. The phone rang. In the kitchen, Hudson dried his hands with a towel, then walked over to her.

The call connected. "Vienna?" Melissa asked. Worry laced her tone. "Where are you?"

"Yes, it's me," she half whispered the words, though it wasn't like anyone was going to overhear except Hudson. "We're on the way to the police, but I had to stop for my data backup at home. I'm so sorry they killed him." Her voice cracked, and she swallowed back tears springing into her eyes.

Sniffling came through the phone, like Melissa was trying to keep herself together. Poor woman. How kind of her to think of Vienna at a time like this. "I know you didn't do it," she said, "no matter what the cops say. Kevin told me you were on to something big. He wouldn't say what, but he said he was afraid someone was trying to steal your work."

That lined up with the concerns she'd heard him express, and the fact he'd wanted to schedule their meeting after work. "Did he know who it was?" she asked. "Did he say anything that might help us figure it out?"

"No," Melissa answered. "But I haven't had time to look through his personal things yet. Maybe there's something in his emails or notes."

"Can you check? I hate to ask you to even think about this right now, but it might help." It might help a ton, at least in terms of clearing her name. But she could hardly press the new widow to start her own investigation.

"I will. And Vienna—" Melissa broke off, going silent for a moment. When she spoke again, her voice was low and ragged. "Be careful who you trust. Even the police. Kevin's been secretive about work projects ever since that fire, like he knew something might happen. I think this runs a whole lot deeper than just you and him. Where should I contact you again, your cell?"

"No, the police have it. I'll give you Hudson's." The words came out as a mere breath, strangled by the fear clotting up her throat. She glanced at Hudson, who leaned against the arm of the couch near her desk. "What's your phone number?" she asked, then repeated the number to Melissa.

"Give her my landline, too," he added, "on Isle Royale. Just in case she needs to get in touch with me after—" He clamped his mouth shut, then told her the number.

After he turns me in to the cops.

Her insides felt cold and hollow as she hung up the phone. If the authorities were compromised in any way, was there a chance they'd destroy her data backup when she was turned in? Or hand it over to the men who were after her? But what could she do?

"What's up? What did she say?" Hudson asked. After Vienna relayed the gist of the conversation, he rubbed a hand over his chin, then pinned her with his cool blue gaze. "I have to take you in to the police. No matter what she told you. I used to know guys on the force here—they'll be able to sort it out."

"You did?" She frowned. He had seemed familiar with the coastline, too. Had he spent time over here before?

He pressed his lips together, like he'd said more than he'd intended, then stood and glanced toward the way they'd come in. "Did you find what you needed? We need to get moving."

Her laptop chimed as the file transfer finished. She clicked the mouse to safely eject the disk and was about to rise when a thought occurred to her. Why not email the data to her old mentor and postdoc boss, Jeremiah Crofton? Jeremiah had spearheaded their end of the research, and he and Kevin Glickman had a long friendship. He probably had no clue yet what had happened, unless the press had leaked the story already.

"I need a few more minutes," she said, clicking open her email app. Composing the message wouldn't take long, and the peace of mind would be worth it. Then at least *someone* she trusted would have the data, in case anything happened to this flash drive.

She was typing so fast, she almost didn't notice the soft thumps reverberating through the floor. So quiet it wasn't a sound, exactly. More like footsteps. She paused, mid-word, and glanced up at Hudson.

From the way he stood—motionless, eyes alert—he'd heard it, too.

Someone was in the house.

Hudson pressed a finger to his lips and pivoted on the ball of his foot. The house had gone silent, but only a moment before he'd felt rhythmic thumps coming through the floor. Footsteps. His hand dropped down to the sidearm at his waist, and he slipped it out of the holster.

How had they gotten inside? He hadn't heard anyone approach the house—no boat engines or motor vehicles—but maybe the running water of the kitchen sink had masked the noise. Vienna had left the garage door open, as they'd only planned on staying inside for a few minutes. Was the intruder in the mudroom? Or had they taken Vienna's keys from her lab and used them to unlock the front door?

He listened, straining to hear any sound that might indicate where the intruder was. Then it came again—soft footfalls coming from the front of the house, down a hallway he assumed led to the front door. His gaze flicked to Vienna's. She pointed to the hall and then downward, mouthing the word *stairs*.

The ground floor sliding door, beneath the deck. Someone must've found a way to work it open without him or Vienna hearing.

He nodded, then gestured at Vienna to stay put as he

worked his way back across the wood floor, testing each step for creaky floorboards with the toe of his boot before putting down his full weight. When he reached the corner where the wall met the hallway, he paused and stole a quick glance around it.

Muted light filtered through glass panes at the top of the front door, barely touching the dark shadows in the corners. No one was there. A railing to the left marked the staircase to the basement, and a door on the right opened into something. A coat closet? A second living room space? He couldn't see from this angle.

After a last glance at Vienna, who could've been a marble statue in her chair, he released the safety on his gun and stepped around the corner, keeping close to the wall. His heartbeat thudded in his ears, far outpacing each cautious step he took. There was no sign of movement, no sound beyond his own breath. Had he only imagined the footsteps earlier?

Then a thump sounded below, coming from the stairs leading to the lower level. The hairs stood up on the back of his neck. No question this time—someone was inside the house. Holding the gun out at arm's length, he peered over the railing. Nothing.

A few more steps took him to the open door on the right. A glance inside revealed a room of empty bookshelves and cardboard boxes Vienna apparently had never quite gotten around to unpacking. Two front-facing windows were darkened by closed wooden blinds. When nothing moved, he continued past the room and pivoted to put his back against the front door with the weapon pointing down the stairs.

More thumps, followed by a muffled sound almost like talking. Maybe whoever was down there didn't realize he and Vienna were inside. Good. He'd have the element of surprise.

He crept down the stairs, placing each foot with painful care and keeping to the side of the steps as much as possible. Ducking low to see beneath the ceiling, he scanned the room below for any sign of the intruder. The stairs led into a small family room, complete with fireplace against the wall on the left and the sliding glass doors to the right, which opened onto a concrete slab beneath the deck above. No one appeared to be hiding behind the couch or other furniture.

The sliding door was ajar, letting in a wailing evergreen-scented breeze that whipped across a stack of magazines lying on an end table. Natural light illuminated the room, but the edges were shrouded in dark shadow. He eased down the last few steps, freezing when the bottom one let out a loud groan.

No one appeared. Where was the intruder? A dark hallway led away from the stairs to the right. Another opened off the family room, probably leading to bedrooms. He'd have to check each room. Better to start with the larger ones.

He'd only made it two steps away from the stairs when glass shattered up above. A woman's scream sliced through the air, freezing his blood. *Vienna*. They must've been waiting up above, on the deck. But before he could dash back up the staircase, a dark mass emerged from the shadows next to the stairs. He turned.

Too slow. There was a loud *thunk*. Pain burst through his skull, and stars filled his vision. His legs collapsed, sending him crashing to the ground.

"Gotcha," a male voice muttered.

As blackness overtook the stars, Hudson realized they'd lured him down here on purpose. He'd been tricked. And now they had Vienna.

SIX

A crow cawed, its harsh cry interfering with the heaviness of Hudson's eyelids. He wanted to sleep for the next fifteen years. But the breeze on his face and the persistent bird call—almost like a warning bell—tugged him into wakefulness. And something else...

Vienna. He bolted upright as the details of the attack flooded back into his brain. The room swayed before his eyes, and he braced a hand against the nearby staircase railing. That had been a doozy of a hit—this pounding headache was all the proof he needed. Gently he prodded the injury with his fingers. Sticky blood matted his hair, but his skull felt okay. No fractures. Any hit hard enough to knock a person out could give you a concussion, though. His gun still lay a few feet away, hidden beneath a small end table. Good thing, too, or the men would have snagged it. He clicked the safety back into place and returned it to its holster.

He wanted to leap up and search for Vienna, but first he forced himself to dig his cell phone out of a pocket and punch in a call to emergency services. As soon as the police and EMTs were on the way, he hauled himself up to his feet using the railing. The room stopped spinning after a few moments, and he worked his way back up the steps.

She was gone. No surprise, but that didn't make his failure hurt any less. Now she and her data had fallen into those men's hands, and who knew what they would do to her. A vice tightened around his ribs, threatening to crush his lungs.

He forced in a deep breath and walked over to her desktop computer. Maybe he could find the files and save them for her somehow. Or make sure the police got the hard drive. The screen was black, but he shook the mouse to see if it was only asleep. Vienna's email app sprang to life. Good—it looked like she'd been able to send whatever message she'd been composing. Her flash drive was gone, but he'd make sure the cops took the hard drive.

But where had the men taken her? And how had they gotten away? By boat or by car? One of the sliding glass doors to the deck had been shattered—the sound he'd heard earlier—testifying to their entrance from that direction. They must have climbed up from the level below. Cautiously he stepped through the broken glass and out onto the deck. A quick scan of the ground revealed trampled grass, but the footprints didn't lead to the lake. Instead, they went around the far side of the house. Had they come via vehicle instead of boat?

His brain still felt sludgy, so he forced himself to walk slowly as he navigated back through the house and out the front door. The path of trampled grass wrapped around to the front, ending at Vienna's gravel driveway. He'd never heard an engine—had they crept down from the main road, then had someone brazenly pick them up in her driveway? The gravel was disturbed here, like someone had braked sharply.

Something black caught his eye at the edge of the gravel, partially obscured by the grass. He walked over and bent to pick it up. Vienna's flash drive. She would never have let that fall by accident. But where had they taken her?

He followed the path of the long driveway up toward the main road, working his way around the trees hemming the edges. At the top, he paused. The gravel had been scattered here, too, in a very noticeable pattern, as if the vehicle had pulled in from the south and backed out the same way again to head north. Where did this road go?

Sirens reached his ears as he pulled up Google Maps on his phone. A police car came into view from the south, followed by an ambulance. He waved them to a stop. The car pulled over to one side and two officers got out, followed by the EMTs.

"Chief Deputy Nielson," said the shorter, stouter of the two cops. "Are you Ranger Lawrence?"

"That's me." Hudson offered his hand, but the deputy's eyes narrowed.

"Mind telling me what you were doing here, instead of taking Ms. Clayton straight to the sheriff's office like we agreed?"

Right, about that… "Of course, I'll be happy to explain." He broke off with a wince, pressing a hand to the side of his head. His head did legitimately hurt, but right now wasn't the time for lengthy explanations—not with those men getting away.

Nielson pursed his lips. "Looks like you'd better save your explanation for the hospital."

Oh, no, he wouldn't be going to the hospital. Not with Vienna in those men's hands. "I'll be fine. They can't have more than a fifteen-or twenty-minute head start. Look at the way the gravel is scattered. Where does this road go?" He pointed to the north, in the direction he thought they'd taken Vienna.

"Loops back up to Highway 61," Nielson said, studying the ground. "Smith, get some pictures of this. I'm going down to the house. Ranger Lawrence, I'll let these folks—" he nodded toward the approaching EMTs "—do their work. We'll take it from here."

"Over here, please, sir," one of the EMTs said, taking his arm. Nielson kept walking, like he hadn't listened to anything Hudson had said.

"Chief Deputy Nielson—" Hudson called.

"We'll handle it," the other officer said. "This is an ongoing investigation, and you don't need to worry about Ms. Clayton."

Ha. He was way too involved now to step away from this case. "You do realize she's innocent, don't you?" Hudson swallowed down the irritation souring his stomach and stood still as one of the EMTs shined a light in his eyes. The other EMT, a woman, wrapped a blood pressure cuff around his arm and placed a pulse oximeter on his finger.

"Vitals look good," the woman said after a few minutes.

"Where were you struck?" asked the male EMT. After Hudson showed him the place, he probed the injury with gloved fingers and asked several questions. Hudson rattled off answers, but inside impatience grew like a rangy weed. Chief Deputy Nielson had yet to reappear, and the other officer was still snapping photographs of the driveway.

"I'm fine," he said after what felt like the hundredth question. "My balance is back, I'm not seeing any stars, every limb is working, there's no nausea. I need to find Vienna."

The two EMTs exchanged a glance. Hudson didn't want to be *that* patient, the ornery one they'd swap stories about later, but every second was precious.

"Listen," he said. "I know all about traumatic head injuries. I'm a park ranger, trained in first aid, and I've helped numerous people before. I promise to get checked out if any symptoms come back. Okay?"

Finally the man nodded. "I don't see any obvious signs of concussion, but since you blacked out for at least a few minutes, you need to take it easy. And do make sure to see a doctor if you have any other symptoms."

"I will," Hudson promised, but his feet were already moving down toward the house and his boat. By the time he reached the front door, Nielson was stepping back out.

"Don't go in there," he said sharply. "It's a crime scene."

Hudson restrained himself from rolling his eyes. If anyone here knew that was a crime scene, it was him. He'd been one of the victims. "Did you find any clues?"

"None that I can discuss at this time."

His jaw ached, and he realized he'd been clenching his teeth. Too bad the officers assigned to this case weren't people he knew. Nielson hadn't been on the force when he worked as a ranger in Superior National Forest. Maybe he could call one of his former fellow rangers and see if they knew who was still around from the "old" days. Amazing how much could change in only two years.

"If the EMTs have released you, I'll need to get your statement," Nielson went on. "And your explanation for this little detour."

Irritation burned in his chest at this delay, but he plowed through a five-minute recap of what had happened, including Vienna's request to save the backup of her data, while Nielson recorded his statement. "Where do you think they've taken her?" he asked when he was done.

Nielson's eyes narrowed a fraction. "Ranger Lawrence, I'm not sure how she managed to convince a law enforcement ranger like yourself not to bring her in straightaway, but we were able to access her cell phone that we recovered from her lab. She had a whole string of text messages arranging a meeting with an unknown buyer for last night. My guess is, when she failed to show, they decided to take matters into their own hands. Ms. Clayton is guilty, and she's gotten herself into this situation. Now, we'll do the best we can to find her and see that justice is served, but you need to let us do our job."

Hold up. They'd found text messages on her phone? None of that added up with what Vienna had told him. Or what they'd gone through. Had those men been chasing her because she'd failed to show for a meeting?

Surely not. No one was that good at acting. She'd been terrified of losing her data and crushed over her boss's death. But until the cops could interview her for themselves, they weren't going to see past the evidence against her.

"All right, Chief Deputy Nielson," he said after a long moment. Better to play along for now. But as soon as he got down to his boat, he'd go after her himself. "I won't let her get the better of me again. Please update me when you can."

The other man watched as he hastened across the driveway and back around the house. There wasn't any time to lose. As soon as he was out of sight of the deck, on the rocky path toward the lake, he pulled out his phone and paused to go through his contacts.

There—Sean Morris. He'd been a forest ranger alongside Hudson back in the days when he and Brittany still lived here. He clicked the green call button and waited as the number rang.

The call connected. "Sean here. Hudson, is that you?"

A twinge of guilt made him swallow. Maybe he'd worked a little *too* hard to forget his old life, to the point of cutting out anyone who remembered Brittany. "Yeah, man, long time no talk."

"How have you been?" Sean's tone was as open and friendly as Hudson remembered, no trace of ill will at being more or less ignored for two years. "I've been praying for you over there on Isle Royale." His friend had always been a strong believer, and right now it showed in his graciousness toward Hudson.

"Thanks, Sean. Listen, I'd love to catch up, but right now I could use your help. Do you know anyone still on the police force in the Cook County Sheriff's Office?"

"You mean my side of the lake? Grand Marais?" Sean asked. "Sure. I transferred over to police work a year ago. What can I do for you?"

Sean was an officer now? *Thank You, Lord.* That was an answer to an unasked prayer if he'd ever heard of one. It didn't take long to run through what had happened over the previous eighteen hours with Vienna. Sean was already aware of the case.

"Yeah, the lab murder was a big deal. I can't really give you information without violating orders." His friend paused, as if considering Hudson's request for more details. "You think they went north? I know that area well. There's a big empty warehouse maybe five miles or so up the coast. Used to be a boat storage facility but part of it burned down last year and they closed it up instead of rebuilding."

That had to be it. He remembered it now—he'd passed it a few times on trips to Grand Portage or Thunder Bay. "Thanks, Sean. Let me know if you hear anything else that might help. I owe you."

"The only thing you owe me is a visit sometime. Be safe, brother. If you hear or see anything suspicious, you call it in, okay? We'll get backup there right away." His friend hung up, and Hudson scrambled down the rocky path the rest of the way to his boat.

As he cranked on the engine and untied the lines, a band cinched around his ribs. So much time had passed already.

Even if he could find Vienna, would he be too late?

Vienna's arms ached from the way they were tied behind her back around the hard plastic chair. And between the faint scent of motor diesel in the air and this filthy rag stuffed in her mouth, it was all she could do not to gag.

They'd taken her to the Superior Marine storage facility north on Highway 61. The place was abandoned now, full of charred remains and twisted metal beams that had collapsed in a fire last year. But the men had found an untouched office at one end of the building, where they'd tied her up and left her. A lone guard paced back and forth outside the office door, visible through the big glass window. Beyond him, the huge metal shelving designed to hold boats rose up like giant skeletons.

She twisted against the ropes, though after half an hour of struggling she knew it was pointless. All she had to show for her efforts were painful rope burns on both arms beneath her fleece pullover. How long were they going to leave her in here? And what were they waiting for?

Voices sounded outside the door, and she stiffened as it opened and two men entered. One was armed, like the guard who remained outside the office, but the other carried a laptop.

Hers.

He swatted away a pile of debris from the old desk in the center of the office, then set the computer on the surface. "Bring her over," he said gruffly.

The other man took the chair and roughly hauled it toward the desk, painfully jolting her neck. She gritted her teeth around the rag, blinking dust out of her eyes. Was there any hope the police were looking for her? And what had happened to Hudson? She hadn't seen him anywhere here. *Please let him be safe, Lord.* He'd gone through enough on her account already.

"All right," said the one who seemed to be in charge. "This is real simple, Ms. Clayton. You access the formula and the data for us, and we let you go. Easy as that."

Dr. *Clayton to you.* But all she could do was scowl at them over the rag stuffed in her mouth.

From the way the two guards smirked at each other across the room, she sincerely doubted they'd ever let her go. Her only hope was to stay alive long enough for Hudson or the police to find her.

If they were even looking.

Despair oozed into her heart like a black fog, but she'd deal with her feelings later. Right now, she had to face these men. She looked at the man with her laptop, right into his cold, brown eyes, and shook her head defiantly.

He frowned. Then he pulled a black object out of his pocket, and with a flick of his wrist and flash of silver, a switchblade popped out. Her chest tightened as he walked over to her.

"Don't make this difficult," he said.

She winced as he moved behind her, preparing for whatever pain would come next, but he merely cut the gag loose. The grimy cloth fell to the floor, and she swallowed a few times in a vain attempt to get moisture back into her mouth.

"Here's the deal," the man said. The blade flashed again, and this time the ropes binding her arms dropped. Other ropes still held her chest and legs into place, but at least she could shake out her hands to get some circulation flowing again. "The boss knows you might not feel like cooperating, so we've got a little incentive."

He held up his cell phone. The screen displayed a list of—she strained to read the text—names and addresses. Of BMRL employees and other people she knew. Melissa Glickman was at the top of the list.

"See that?" He tapped on the phone again, then held up what looked like a video feed of a lovely two-story home, spring flowers blooming in front of the brick facade. She recognized it right away from work holiday parties—it was the Glickmans' home. "This is a live feed, from our operative parked outside Melissa Glickman's house. She's in her kitchen right now, washing dishes." His lip curled into an ugly sneer. "She won't be for long, if you don't tell us what we want to know."

Vienna's heart sank into her toes. Dr. Glickman had lost his life in their secret meeting intended to protect this research. And now, she had to choose between saving his life's work or saving his wife.

But what choice was there, with Melissa's life in danger?

She gritted her teeth and reached for the computer, avoiding the man's cruel gaze. "All right. I'll give you what you want." Her only hope now was to stall as long as possible.

"Good choice." He shoved her chair closer to the desk, so that her fingers could reach the keypad.

After opening her work laptop, she placed her thumb on the power button to activate the fingerprint scanner. The screen lit up as the computer booted. "What do you want from me?" she asked. If only this machine had a slower start-up time. But unfortunately all the icons were already on the screen.

"The correct formula. And the data set that proves it."

She lifted a finger to point at the screen. "It's right he—"

"No. In a new folder, on that side so we can see it." He gestured toward an empty part of the screen, where the background image of a rocky coast and crashing waves was easily visible.

Vienna right clicked on the background, creating a new folder and taking her sweet time typing in a name for it. She could lie…drag the wrong data set into the folder. How would he know the difference? Her finger hovered over the mouse as she scanned the files on the screen, biting her lip.

"Hurry it up," the man barked. "And don't even think about cheating, unless you don't want to see Melissa Glickman again."

So much for that idea. A small sigh escaped as she dragged the correct files over to the folder. Years of effort and work, gone in the blink of an eye. It was hard to understand why God would ever let this happen. How was this going to work out for the good?

After Jack had told her he wanted a divorce, she'd poured herself into this work. Finding a new way to treat antibiotic-resistant bacteria became her purpose in life, the thing that saved her after the shame and heartache of her failed marriage. She'd seen so many tragic stories on the news, heard of so many painful, unnecessary deaths that could have been prevented with this new medicine.

Why would God pull away His blessing now, when she and her lab were so close to success? She bit back tears.

But her captor had no interest in the dark night of her soul. "Done?" he demanded. When she nodded, he clapped the laptop shut and pulled it away. Then he walked toward the door, leaving her behind with the armed guard.

"Wait," she called. "You said you'd let me go."

He stopped in the doorway and looked back. "Not until I

share these files with the boss." His lips curled into a sneer. "Then we'll set you free."

When the guard behind her laughed harshly, every suspicion she'd had was confirmed. She may have saved Melissa's life, but not her own.

They intended to kill her.

SEVEN

Hudson cut the boat's engine and hopped onto the dock. He'd chosen a stretch at the far south end of the empty marina, beneath the windowless, intact wall of the huge white and blue warehouse looming above. It would've been better to dock out of sight completely, but the rocky coastline to the south offered no good alternatives.

He drew his gun, double-checked the magazine and jogged across the dock. There was no sign of movement up above. Hopefully that meant the only guards were inside, not patrolling the perimeter. From the encounter at Vienna's house, he knew there had to be at least two, but more likely three or four, people involved. Probably all armed, and without any inhibitions when it came to shooting. As soon as he could confirm Vienna's presence, he'd notify Sean. His friend could handle telling Nielson and sending reinforcements.

Gravel crunched beneath his boots as he reached the rocky beach. He kept low to the ground, constantly scanning for any sign of motion, but there was nothing. When he reached the wall of the building, he crept along it to the east corner, then peered around. The marina spread out to the right, with the blue lake glistening beneath the midday sun beyond. Ahead, the white, corrugated metal wall of the building stretched on for maybe a hundred feet before it collapsed into a mound of debris left over from the fire. Metal beams rose like black bones stretching for the sky, and jagged sheets of twisted metal intertwined with the hollowed-out shells of destroyed boats.

There'd be no easy way to enter from that direction. If the men were holding Vienna inside, they'd have to be in the intact end, maybe even in an attached office. He turned and jogged west, heading for the other corner of the building. On this side, a section of the building jutted out toward the parking lot, with a sidewalk stretching like a concrete snake across the green lawn. Windows glistened in the sunshine, and a blue awning over the entrance greeted visitors. This part of the building had obviously survived the fire. And it looked a lot more like the place where he would find Vienna.

He scanned the parking lot and surrounding woods, looking for any sign of movement. No guards appeared to be on patrol, but a splash of white between the trees caught his eye. A gravel service road led away from the parking lot and into the forest on the right. That had to be where they'd stowed their vehicle.

Keeping low against the wall, he scurried forward until he was crouched beneath one of the windows in the building's extension. There was space between two of the windows to stand, so he rose to his feet, staying as close against the wall as he could. With his gun at the ready, he dared a quick glance inside. The glare off the glass made it nearly impossible to see inside, but he could just make out what looked like an entryway with a receptionist's desk.

He crouched down again and ducked beneath the windows to reach the front of the building. The blue awning overhead draped the glass front door and windows on this side in shadows. From his position at the corner, he could easily see into the front door now. No one appeared to be inside. More windows beyond the door must look into another room, maybe office space.

After darting past the glass door, he crouched beneath the first window and scanned his surroundings again. The parking lot was still empty, but glimpses of white showed through the trees down that gravel road. If it was their vehicle, it hadn't moved. He was about to stand up to glance through the window when he heard voices coming from inside farther down. Crouching low, he crept beneath the glass panes until he could hear the sounds more distinctly, stopping at the far corner.

From here, the rest of the warehouse was visible. Like the other side, the walls stretched on for a bit before dissolving into charred ruins. A quick glance around the corner showed the nearest window glass on this side had cracked and fallen out, maybe damage from the heat. That had to be where the voices were coming from. He inched forward, moving slowly to avoid making noise, then stopped to listen.

"Boss says the data looks good." A male voice, and based on the tone, not the one who'd knocked him out earlier. "Glad it wasn't up to me. I ain't no scientist."

"Ha, that's for sure," a second man grunted. He sounded a whole lot more like Hudson's old friend with the blunt object. Just hearing the man's voice made the injury throb. "What about the woman?"

Hudson gritted his teeth. They had to be talking about Vienna. He pulled out his phone and shot off a text to Sean. Backup would be here in a matter of minutes.

"We don't need her anymore. Boss says to make it look like a deal gone wrong," the man said.

"But you said—" A loud smack cut off Vienna's voice. They'd hit her. Red hazed across his vision. Suddenly all he wanted was to charge in, take out those men and get her to safety. But being reckless would only get them killed.

"Enough!" the first man barked. "Here's the plan. We shoot her in the chest, then untie the ropes and take them with us. Then wipe the gun of prints and leave it here for the cops to find. They'll trace it back to whoever the boss set up as the buyer. Got it?"

"Got it." Oh, that sounded like a *third* man.

A vice gripped Hudson's chest. Waiting for backup was out of the question, but he and Vienna were outnumbered and outgunned. Only the element of surprise was on their side.

And their Heavenly Father. *Please, protect us, Lord.*

He'd barely had time to think the prayer when a click sounded—a gun's safety being switched off. There was no time left to consider or to plan, only to act.

Hudson sprang to his feet, planting his free hand onto the windowsill in a space without visible glass shards, and using the momentum to fling his legs up and into the room. The next few seconds happened in a fragmented blur. Vienna's face startled into utter shock at his appearance. Several voices shouting at once. His elbow connecting with the head of the nearest man.

The man slumped to the ground. Hudson dove for the floor, rolling across it as a shot fired at the spot where he'd just been standing. He landed on his back on the floor behind Vienna. She was tied to a chair, but somehow her arms were free. She grabbed onto the edge of the desk in front of her and jerked her chair sideways, out of his firing range. Smart woman.

Hudson's gun cracked as he shot at an armed man on

the other side of the desk. The man crashed to the floor, falling backward like he'd been struck in the shoulder. A third man, who must've been unarmed, dove for the gun the other man had dropped.

"Hudson!" Vienna called, her voice laced with panic.

The first guard he'd taken down was starting to stir. "Here," he said, pressing the gun into her hands. "Shoot if you have to, just not at me."

Her eyes went wide but she nodded, swiveling the gun toward the man. Working quickly, he tugged a pocketknife out of his utility belt and cut the ropes binding her back and ankles to the chair. A shot sounded and he ducked. The man on the other side of the desk.

Vienna screamed, tumbling from the chair. As she landed, her finger pulled the trigger, firing a blast at the ceiling. Fragments of ceiling tile rained down over their heads.

His chest constricted. Had she been shot?

"Vienna!" he launched for the gun, snatching it from the floor where she'd dropped it. Her fleece pullover had a ragged gash on one arm. A trace of red seeped through, but it wasn't gushing. That was a good sign.

She pushed herself up onto her knees. "I'm okay."

A gun fired again, the bullet pinging off the underside of the desk and splintering the wood into a shower of splinters. Hudson fired back, more to keep the man down than to try to hit him.

Something crashed against his back, sending him staggering into the desk. Hudson shoved off from the wood, spinning to land a punch in his attacker's stomach. It was the first guard he'd taken down, now fully awake again. But the man had left his gun where it'd fallen on the ground, and now Vienna dove for it. As her hands latched around the gun, the man launched himself at Hudson, tackling him to the ground. Vienna rolled out of the way, but as soon as she cleared the edge of the desk, the other man fired at her. She screamed.

"Get out of here!" Hudson grunted at her, struggling to keep his gun out of the man's grasp. They rolled across the ground, wrestling, until Hudson finally landed on top and smashed the butt of his gun into the man's face. He shoved to his feet. "Vienna, go!"

The gun felt cold and hard in her hands, like a block of dry ice Vienna had no business holding. Her arm ached, too, so badly she couldn't hold the weapon up unless she used both hands. Hudson was yelling at her to go, but there was still the man with the gun on the other side of the desk. And her laptop, wherever he'd taken it outside of this room. Maybe she could still get it back.

The shooting had stopped while Hudson wrestled with the guard, but now gunfire cracked again, so loud her ears felt like they would never stop ringing. She scuttled around the end of the desk, pressing herself against the wood. The door couldn't be more than eight feet away from where she now crouched, but the man Hudson had shot in the shoulder wasn't there anymore. He must've crawled out.

Then suddenly the desk behind her moved as Hudson shoved the entire thing across the floor, ramming it into the man who'd been firing at them. The man toppled backward, firing stray shots that went wide as he lost his balance.

Keeping her head low, she darted for the door, Hudson hard on her heels. They burst out into a wide aisle between two huge sets of dry storage racks.

"That way," he huffed, pointing past the rack on the left toward the place where the wall had collapsed, revealing blue sky above the blackened piles of debris. He veered over to the lowest rack and jumped up onto the wood planking.

Vienna followed, glancing back over her shoulder before she stepped up. The man with the injured shoulder was nowhere to be seen, but as she watched, the other two came charging out of the office. Blood poured down one of their faces—Hudson must've broken his nose—but that didn't stop him sprinting across the concrete floor in their direction.

"Hurry!" she yelled, scrambling up after Hudson. Shots rang out, firing wildly in their direction. Wood splintered fifteen feet away where the shooter hit the wooden shelf. Hudson pushed her ahead of him, guiding her down off the shelf and back onto the hard concrete floor. Debris from the fire cluttered the aisle on this side. They dodged jagged scraps of metal and hulking lumps of burned-out fiberglass boat hulls as they raced for the broken wall at the far end.

Her breath came in ragged gasps, and she nearly went down on a piece of fallen beam, but Hudson grabbed her arm and tugged her forward. Finally, they climbed out over the last of the debris and onto the gravel bed lining the edge of the warehouse. The waters of Lake Superior gleamed with the promise of escape.

"There!" Hudson yelled, pointing at his boat where it bobbed at the end of a long dock. They took off at a full sprint. Every moment Vienna expected to feel the bite of a bullet in her back, but none came. When they reached the dock and she finally dared to glance back, there was no trace of movement.

"Do you…think…we lost them?" she huffed out between gasps for air.

"I hope so." Hudson hopped over the gunwale and cranked on the boat's engine.

She pulled loose the stern and bow lines and climbed in after him. As the boat motored away, the whine of sirens drifted down from the coastal highway up above. She stood next to him beneath the canopy, watching as red and blue lights flashed through the trees and turned into the bit of parking lot visible from this side of the building.

"Cops are there," she said, then instantly regretted her words. What if Hudson wanted to take her back? Turn her in? If the men had heard the police coming and managed to get away with her laptop, what evidence would she have that they were trying to frame her? "Please don't take me back."

He wiped the back of his hand across his forehead, then fixed her with his crystal blue eyes, as if he were reading her very soul. His gaze darted to the shredded sleeve of her fleece, where the ache had dulled slightly and rusty red crusted the ragged fabric. "Are you all right?"

Something about his expression tugged at her insides in a way that made her want to squirm. It'd been a long time since a man had looked at her that way. Not since she and Jack had been dating, when he'd gone out of his way to make sure she felt cared for. But of course, Hudson wasn't thinking anything along those lines, he was just doing his job.

"Yes," she said, glancing down at the ripped sleeve of her fleece. "One of the bullets clipped me but I think it's only a graze."

He studied her a moment longer, then nodded. And cranked up the speed of the motor. "Sure is hard to hear over this engine," he yelled, louder than necessary. "I'll be sure to explain that to the cops when I give my testimony."

She stared at him for a moment, her brows pinching together. Then his lips cracked into a grin, and she laughed. "Thank you." Warmth bloomed in her chest. What had she done to deserve his help? *Nothing*. All she'd done was put him in danger. And yet she was so utterly grateful to him, and to the Lord for not letting her face this situation alone.

Light danced in his blue eyes the same way it did on the lake's waves. He was kind, this man she'd just met. And very capable.

When he looked away to check the instrument panel, heat burned up the back of her neck. What was she doing, staring into his eyes?

He cleared his throat. "I overheard those men talking about how their boss had set you up to be framed. I know you're innocent. But I also know that the police have procedures they've got to follow, and that it'll be a lot harder to clear your name if you're in jail. Besides…" His lips pressed together as he studied her again. "You don't want to be in jail."

"No. I don't. But what do we do now?" She watched the coastline shrink as they headed away from it, farther out into the lake. She'd assumed at first that his goal was to make sure the men lost visual contact, just in case they were watching, and that then he'd turn southwest and take her back to Grand Marais. But now that he was going to help her, where could they go? "I was able to send a partial email to my old mentor, Dr. Crofton, but those men broke into my house before I could attach the data set. I only had time to hit Send. It would be best if I could get in contact with him to explain."

"If it's okay with you," he went on, "I think it's best if we return to Isle Royale. It'll be easier to lie low while you get in touch with Dr. Crofton and we figure out a plan. Oh, and I found this on the ground outside your house." He reached into his pocket and then held out his hand, her black flash drive resting on his palm.

She smiled. "Thank you." She slipped it into her pocket. Going back to Isle Royale sounded appealing, but what about the part where the other rangers saw her led off in handcuffs earlier? How would Hudson explain? "Will there be a problem for you, bringing me back there instead of to the police?"

He shook his head. "Not with what went down at the warehouse. Chief Ranger Dietz is the down-to-earth, common-sense type. He'll get it. In fact—" he reached for the boat's radio "—I should update him now."

Static crackled as he called the Isle Royale dispatcher and asked to be patched through to the chief ranger. The interchange was brief and to the point, explaining what had happened at the warehouse and how Hudson wanted to bring Vienna back to Isle Royale overnight, keeping her whereabouts on the down low until he could make sure she was safe.

"Dietz will buy us some time with the sheriff's office," he said once he had signed off, "but it'd be better if no one saw you when we get back to Windigo. The fewer people who know you're there, the better." He scanned her for a moment, then turned his attention back to the steering. "We need to check that wound, too, as soon as we're out of sight of the coast."

Fifteen minutes later, he set the engine to idle and let the boat rock gently on the water. Vienna tugged her good arm out of the fleece while he pulled out a first aid kit. The other arm was more difficult—the blood had dried now, crusting onto the fabric of her fleece and the shirt beneath.

Hudson frowned as he examined it, then pulled out a pair of scissors. "We have to cut the fabric. I'm sorry."

"It can't be helped." She did her best to hold still as he

exposed the wound. As she'd suspected, the bullet had only grazed her, but the gash still made her stomach turn.

She clenched her teeth as he squirted clean water from a bottle over the injury, washing away the dried blood and bits of fabric. Isopropyl alcohol came next, burning so badly she cried out in pain.

Hudson winced. "I know it hurts."

Then an antibiotic spray, and finally sterile gauze and bandaging. With her sleeve in tatters and her arm wrapped, she felt like she'd been through a war zone. And they weren't close to being done yet, not until she could make sure her data was in good hands and figure out who was after her.

The sun was dipping toward the west by the time land came into view. Vienna rose from her seat to stand next to Hudson. She glanced at the instrument panel. Nearing 4:00 p.m., according to the clock.

"Is that Isle Royale?" she asked, pointing toward the distant coastline.

"It is." He grew silent almost immediately, a muscle working in his jaw. Now that they were almost back, she couldn't help worrying. What if the chief ranger changed his mind, and Hudson got into trouble?

"I'm sorry," she said. "I shouldn't have let you bring me back here. I don't want to cause more trouble for you."

He slowed the boat's engine and turned to face her. "Vienna, don't apologize. This was my choice, and I'm doing it because I believe you. Right now, the police don't know what happened to either of us. They're not expecting you to turn up here. The chief will update them if necessary, but it won't hurt to let them wait a few hours so you can make sure your data is safe.

"Now—" he increased the speed again "—here's the

plan. I'll need to return the boat keys, but I'll try to avoid any conversations. The rangers in Windigo won't have heard about the attack yet, nor will they know you're still with me. In the meantime, you can head straight for my cabin and use my computer to access your email."

She nodded, struck again by the beauty of the island as they made the turn into the big harbor. Rocky shore gave way to tall pine trees above shimmering blue water. The remoteness made it even more stunning. It was one of those places she dreamed about visiting, or even living in—but not sneaking into as a wanted suspect. Maybe one day she'd make it back here.

Her gaze caught on Hudson as she scanned the horizon. The wind scattered blond hair across his forehead, but his attention to the water never wavered, and his hands were strong and adept on the boat's wheel. He looked every inch a park ranger, like he'd been born and raised on this island. So different than her ex-husband.

She still wasn't sure what had ever made her think marrying Jack was a good idea. They'd always been polar opposites, except for their love of science. Even that had been a sham though, as she'd figured out too late. So many things that she'd believed to be true about him ended up being wrong.

Was that the case for all men? Was it impossible to know someone well enough to make a good decision about a life together?

Or—the thought speared her insides—had it been her fault? Maybe Jack had never meant her to think all those things about him, but she'd romanticized the relationship and missed all the obvious signs. Maybe *she* hadn't been who he'd thought either. And then, when he'd realized she wasn't what he wanted, he'd dropped her.

Well, that was never going to happen again. Because science didn't break up with you for not meeting expectations, the way people did. She'd learned her lesson. Her focus now was on her work, not relationships.

The boat bumped against the dock, jolting her from her thoughts.

Hudson turned to her. "My cabin is straight up the hill behind the visitor center, farthest one on the left. Number seven. Here." He pressed a key ring into her hands. "You go on ahead. I'll meet you there in fifteen minutes. The computer password is hashtag Romans eight two eight, capital *R*. Good?"

"Yeah, I'll remember." The verse popped immediately into her mind. *And we know that all things work together for good to them that love God...* Funny, that they had this in common. "That's my favorite verse," she added, almost mumbling it, but the crooked grin that appeared on his face told her he'd heard. She wrapped stiff fingers around the keys and climbed out of the boat. Then she walked briskly up the dock.

No one was out here, but every window glistening in the sinking sun could've been a shining eye staring at her. She kept her head down and hurried up the hill away from the lake, despite the exhaustion dragging at her heavy limbs. Hard to believe they'd pulled in here for the first time only this morning. It'd been less than twenty-four hours since the incident at her lab.

She shivered, trying to unsee Dr. Glickman slumped over that conference table, or the cruel way those men had looked at her in the warehouse. Cabins appeared in the woods through the path ahead, temporarily erasing the painful images. Turning left, she jogged lightly down the path until she reached number seven. The place was buried back in the woods, nearly invisible from the rest of the group. Had Hudson requested this one, or was it the only one available? He didn't seem like a social recluse—he'd been friendly and kind to his coworkers and to her—but there *was* something about the man that made him hard to get to know. Like he kept the inner part of himself tucked away where no one could access it.

It took a few attempts to find the right key, but then the lock clicked open and she stepped inside. The place had a warm, cozy feel, with its knotted pine floors and walls, wood-burning stove and wool throws on the furniture. Large windows made the small space feel like an extension of the outside, where a blend of pine and deciduous trees cocooned the cabin. A soft scent of smoke from the stove mingled with coffee and evergreen.

As much as she wanted to curl up under one of those blankets and sleep for a decade, she forced her tired feet over to the desk against the opposite wall. Doors leading off the main room opened into a tiny kitchen and a hallway with what looked like a single bathroom and bedroom. Small, but…perfect, really.

The computer screen flicked on when she shook the mouse, and she typed in the password, letting God's promise in that verse wash over her again. Somehow, God would work all these horrible things together for the good. Maybe it wasn't something she'd see or understand in this lifetime, but He was trustworthy. He knew what He was doing.

Comforted by the thought, she drew in a slow breath and opened her email. Her heart skipped—Dr. Crofton had responded, less than thirty minutes ago. Vienna, are you okay? Please tell me what's going on.

She typed back a short message, praying he would be online and see it right away even though it was a Saturday.

They needed to *talk*, but without her own phone, a Zoom call would be the most efficient. And then Dr. Crofton could see for himself that she was in earnest.

Ten minutes later, as she was resting with her head on the crook of her arm, a soft knock sounded at the door. She leaped up, disoriented for a minute, then remembered where she was. When she pulled the door open, Hudson slipped inside.

"Everything go okay?" she asked. Worry pulled at her insides, both that she'd get him in trouble and that she'd be arrested again before talking to Dr. Crofton.

"Yeah. The only person I saw was the ranger on duty when I returned the boat keys, and she was some college kid who wouldn't know about your arrest. Knew about last night's boat chase, though." His lips tilted into a wry grin as he shrugged.

"I emailed Dr. Crofton," she said, leading the way back to the computer. Good, he'd responded and sent a Zoom link. "Do you have Zoom on here?"

"Sure. The internet isn't very fast, but it should work." He helped her set up the camera and connect the audio, then stepped back as Dr. Crofton waved at her. "I'm going to clean up and brew some coffee. Holler if you need anything."

"Thanks." She turned back to the screen. Her former postdoc mentor, Jeremiah Crofton, was in his midfifties now. His dark hair was streaked with silver, and worry lines creased his forehead.

"I got your email, Vienna," he said, "but it cut off midsentence. What's going on?"

She went through the entire story, starting with her after-work meeting with Dr. Glickman. The video feed froze periodically, but the audio connection was fine. Her voice caught as she described the gunman bursting into the room and shooting him. Dr. Crofton pressed a hand to his mouth as he listened. She wrapped up with how Hudson had helped her escape the warehouse, but she'd given up the formula and the dataset to protect Melissa.

Dr. Crofton nodded, his lips pressed together in a firm line. "You made the right choice, contacting me. Kevin told me about the fire at BMRL. He was convinced it wasn't an accident."

"He was?" she asked. He'd never said that to her.

"He didn't want to scare any of you, but after that he suspected someone was far too interested in this project." Dr. Crofton glanced to the side, like he was looking at something across the room, then turned back to her. "Can you get the data uploaded to me now?"

"I'll try," she promised. "The internet here isn't the greatest. I'm on Isle Royale with a ranger who's helping me."

"Yes, do your best. I'll make sure it stays safe until we're ready to move forward with the project again. And in the meantime, I've got a couple of leads to look into. Kevin mentioned another company he suspected of trying to steal trade secrets."

He paused, looking away again, almost as if he'd heard a noise. The background behind him didn't appear to be his office at Johns Hopkins. Instead, the low bookcases and framed art indicated a home office. His wife had passed a few years before Vienna had met him. Was there someone else visiting his home?

"Who was it?" she asked. The picture froze.

"What?" He looked at her again as the feed came back, his eyebrows pulling together.

"The name of the company," she pressed.

He opened his mouth as if to answer, but no sound came out.

"You're breaking u—"

Dr. Crofton jerked suddenly to one side, clutching his chest. A look of horror spread across his face as he turned to something off-screen she couldn't see. Then another jolt, and through the glitching video feed she watched him fall sideways off his chair, out of her field of vision.

"Dr. Crofton! Jeremiah!" she yelled, as if somehow she could jump through the screen and help him. What had happened?

Then a man appeared in front of the camera, a black mask covering his face. He held a piece of paper up in front of the screen, two words scrawled on it with a black Sharpie. A few seconds later, she was kicked out of the Zoom meeting.

But those two words stayed etched on her retinas.

You're next.

EIGHT

At the sound of Vienna's muffled scream coming from the living room, Hudson dropped the towel he'd been using to dry his hair and dashed out of the bathroom. He found her where he'd left her, sitting in front of the computer, but the Zoom window was now gone.

She turned to face him, the whites of her eyes huge around her dark brown irises. "Jeremiah Crofton… They… He's…" Each word came out between a gasp for air, like she was struggling to breathe.

He crouched down next to her, placing a hand on her knee. "Did something happen?"

She nodded. Then sucked in a couple of rapid gasps. "Someone broke into his house during our meeting. I think… I think they may have killed him."

Hudson exhaled sharply. That was *not* good news. How far did this criminal network extend? "Where was he, Vienna? Close to BMRL?"

"No. Johns Hopkins. Maryland."

He rose to his feet and paced back and forth near the desk. "How did they know where to find him? Or get there so quickly?"

"They must've seen my email open on my desktop computer earlier and checked the sent messages. He's a public figure—faculty at Johns Hopkins. His address would be easy to find. And if they were already watching him the way they're watching Melissa Glickman…because of his connection to me…" Her words faded away until he could hardly hear her. "It's my fault. Hudson, it's my fault if he's dead."

He strode over to her, placing both of his hands on her shoulders. "*None* of this is your fault. You've only been doing your job. And trying to help the rest of humanity in the process. You can't blame yourself for other people's evil actions."

Her eyes filled with tears, and she tucked in her upper lip. But after a moment, she nodded and he dropped his hands. "He said Dr. Glickman had told him he suspected another company of trying to steal our trade secrets. He was just about to give me the name. And Hudson, whoever killed him held up a message for me."

"What did it say?" He ground the words out, past the anger burning in his esophagus. No one should have to witness all these deaths or feel so threatened just because they wanted to help others.

"You're next." She blinked rapidly, but a lone tear escaped and tracked down her cheek. "We need to notify the authorities out there." Her words came out thick, like they were clotting in her throat.

He gently wiped the tear away with his thumb, holding her sad gaze for a long moment. Then, before he quite knew what he was doing, he pulled her to her feet. "Come here," he said and tugged her into an embrace.

She placed her head against his shoulder and cried, her back shaking, tears soaking into his shirt.

"Shh," he said. "It's okay." The words felt hollow and meaningless in the face of what she'd already gone through, but he had to offer her whatever he could. So he began to pray. "Father in Heaven, we lift this tragedy up to You. These sorrows that feel too overwhelming to bear. You who are sovereign over all things, please be with us now. Strengthen and guide us. Work even these things to the good, even when we can't see a way."

He released her when she pushed away, and she stood sniffling and wiping her cheeks with her sleeve. "Thank you." Then her gaze found his, her eyes so deep a man could fall into them and lose himself completely. "I mean it. Thank you. For everything."

"Of course. I'll get in touch with the Baltimore police and leave an anonymous tip, so we don't attract more attention." Then he gestured to the bathroom. Poor woman looked exhausted. "You can freshen up in there if you'd like. I can get you a clean T-shirt and one of my sweat-shirts." He gestured at her fleece, where her bandaged shoulder was clearly visible through the big hole he'd had to cut. "Let me check that wound before you cover it back up, though."

"That'd be great."

He grabbed one of his newer hoodies from his closet and handed it to her, along with a T-shirt and a clean towel. "Sorry, it'll be huge on you."

"But it won't have holes." She smiled.

After she'd vanished into the bathroom, he rummaged in his kitchen to find anything decent to feed a guest for din-ner. By the time he'd settled on grilled chicken and started some potatoes baking, Vienna reappeared. He had to admit, the burgundy T-shirt with a picture of Michigan's Upper Peninsula on it was the perfect color on her, highlighting her smooth skin and glossy dark hair. She looked like she belonged out here in the woods.

He shook off the errant thought before anything suspicious appeared on his face. "Let me grab the first aid kit."

When he returned from the closet with the plastic case, she was sitting at his tiny kitchen table gazing out the window in the back door.

She glanced up as he entered the room. "Your view of the woods is beautiful."

"Yes, it is." He set the case on the table, then pulled up the other chair. She smelled fresh, like peppermint and sunshine, and he caught himself inhaling a little more deeply than necessary. *Focus.* "Let's have a look at this. Does it hurt?"

"A little." She swallowed and turned back to the window, as if she didn't want to watch, but her chin stayed level. A visual reminder of her inner strength.

Slowly he rolled up her shirt sleeve and peeled back the medical tape holding the wet gauze in place. She'd freshened up and cleaned away some of the blood underneath, revealing an unhappy, two-inch-long graze. After pulling on a fresh pair of gloves, he poked gently at the wound. She inhaled sharply but held still.

"I'm sorry," he said. "I have to make sure it's clean."

"I know." She glanced between the wound and his face, and his breath caught as their gazes met. He hadn't realized exactly how close they were sitting. "Does it need stitches?" she asked. The words came out almost in a whisper.

He shook his head, breaking the moment. Good grief, he was supposed to be cleaning a wound, not staring into her eyes. "It's not deep," he said briskly, grasping for any semblance of a professional tone. "The most important thing will be to keep it clean and covered so you don't get an infection while the skin heals."

Using a squirt bottle from the first aid kit, he washed

the wound again, then sprayed it with a numbing antiseptic. After patting the surrounding skin dry, he re-covered it with clean gauze and taped it into place. Then nearly jumped out of his chair to create some space between them.

"Here, we should keep these handy in case we need to change that bandage," he said, setting some extra gauze packets and the medical tape on the table. While he repacked the rest of the kit, Vienna rolled down her sleeve and slipped the blue hoodie he'd loaned her over her head. Dutifully she tucked the gauze and tape into her front pocket.

"I just need to throw this chicken on the grill—" he pointed to the back door of the cabin "—and then we'll be ready to eat."

He needed a moment alone. To collect himself. Because the effect she had on him… It was trouble. After everything he'd suffered when Brittany died, he could *not* risk getting that close to someone again. There was a reason he'd moved out here to Isle Royale and cut off almost all contact with his old life: he didn't like emotional pain. She'd been hurt, too—of *all* people, shouldn't she understand?

But she followed him to the screen door and leaned against the frame, watching him from inside.

"It's so peaceful out here," she said, her voice irritatingly calm. Soothing. A sound he could keep listening to all night, which made him all the more agitated. "But very isolating, I'd think."

Was it that different than her house? All alone on that rocky hill? They both seemed to share the same taste in housing. "Means no one will notice the smoke from the grill," he said lightly. "Being isolated has its perks."

Like not having people intruding into your personal life.

"Did you pick this cabin? Or did they assign it to you?" She was hard to see through the screen, in the shadows, but he could make out the tilt of her head. Like she was trying to puzzle him out.

Maybe if he was forthright now, she'd get the hint and understand that he worked alone, and that was the way he liked it. "I picked it. I *enjoy* being by myself." The words came out more brusquely than he'd intended, but how exactly could you push another person away without offending them? Didn't it go with the territory?

"Right. I'll check these potatoes." She pushed off from the door frame and vanished into the kitchen.

Leaving him exactly the way he wanted to be—alone. Maybe he'd been a bit harsh a moment ago, but she needed to understand where he was coming from. He'd tried marriage. Settling down into a cute suburban home and a nice church. All he and Brittany had been missing were the two point five children and a dog. And look where that American dream had landed him.

A widower. Alone. In pain, angry at God.

No, he wasn't choosing that road again. Ever.

Still, guilt nagged like a bee sting.

"*Your* house isn't exactly in the center of town," he called in through the open door, trying to sound casual. He flipped over the pieces of chicken with a little more force than necessary.

Inside, the oven door creaked open. Then closed. A moment later, Vienna reappeared at the screen door. "No, it isn't. You're right. But… I needed some space. And I grew up in coastal Maine, so I've always wanted a place like that."

His mind latched on to those words in the middle. *I needed some space.* What had happened? Why was *she* all alone? He hadn't known her long, but anyone could see she was brilliant. And beautiful. Kind. Her concern for him, and her tears for her mentor, proved that. *And* she was a woman of faith. Why hadn't some intelligent guy won her heart by now?

"Makes sense," he said. "So, if you did your postdoc at Johns Hopkins, where were you for your PhD?"

"Boston. MIT."

He waited for more, but she didn't say anything else. Almost like there was something she didn't want to share about, some secret hurt she'd walled up. Not unlike him and Brittany. Maybe they had even more in common than he thought.

"I've never been out there," he said as he pulled the chicken off the grill and slid it onto a plate. The mouth-watering scent of perfectly grilled meat filled the air. At least they wouldn't starve. Maybe they'd even get some sleep tonight.

"Oh, that smells so good." Vienna pressed a hand to her chest and looked longingly at the plate as he carried it past her and into the kitchen.

The potatoes were done, too, and she had somehow cobbled together enough fresh produce to make a salad. A few minutes later, they sat down at his tiny kitchen table. After he prayed to bless the meal, they dug in. The thought struck him that he hadn't sat down to a meal in his home with a woman since Brittany. It felt strange and yet somehow perfectly natural at the same time, being here with Vienna.

Brittany had been more tied to the city than he had ever been. She'd felt safer with modern conveniences close at hand, to the point that she'd rather them both make long commutes than give up their suburban home in Grand Marais.

That home was gone now, though. The thought made his mouth go dry, and he took a sip of his water. "So, tell me again what your former boss said about the lab. He told you Kevin suspected another company was trying to steal from you all?"

Her brows pinched together, and with a start, he realized he'd just given too much away. "You mean Dr. Glickman?" she asked. "Did you know him?"

Too late to backtrack now. He cleared his throat. "Um, yeah, I met him a few times."

She studied him for a moment, but when he didn't elaborate, she said, "Apparently he suspected the fire two years ago wasn't an accident. That someone's been trying to steal from us for a few years now. Dr. Crofton was just about to give me a name when the intruder broke in and attacked him."

Wait, Kevin had believed the fire wasn't an accident? The food in Hudson's mouth turned to ash. He coughed, then grabbed his water and gulped it to cover his reaction. He'd never said anything about it to Hudson, but then Hudson hadn't stuck around long after Brittany's death.

Then a horrifying thought struck him—Brittany was in the lab that night. Why? Had she been involved in this conspiracy somehow?

Vienna sat back from her half-eaten dinner, her arms crossed. Like she knew something was up. Her next words confirmed it. "You told me you knew Brittany Warners, the scientist who died. And you apparently knew Dr. Glickman. What are you *not* telling me?"

He leaned forward, propping his elbows on the table and scrubbing a hand over his face. Maybe Vienna needed to know. Holding back this information was only hindering their efforts.

"Hudson, the only way I'm going to be able to clear my name is to figure out who's after me. If you know something, you have to tell me. Otherwise, why are you helping me?"

Air siphoned out from between his lips in a long sigh. "I'm sorry. I didn't think—I didn't expect there to be so many connections between us." Part of him regretted ever offering to help her, and yet... He couldn't look across the table into those deep brown eyes and not feel like he'd give anything to keep her safe. It was time to come clean.

"Brittany Warners was my wife."

Vienna jerked upright in her chair, any feelings of exhaustion vanishing at Hudson's quiet words. Questions flooded her mind, but instead of pressing him, she leaned forward and rested an arm on the table.

"Warners was her maiden name," he went on. "We met in undergrad, and she'd already had papers published when we got married, so she kept her last name." Not uncommon for female scientists. Vienna had done the same.

He pushed around the food on his plate, as if he needed to keep his hands occupied. "I did a master's in forestry while she earned her MS in biochemistry. Then we moved up to Grand Marais, where I took a job as a forest ranger in Superior National Forest. Brit got the job at BMRL." A soft smile spread across his face, as if he were lost in memories. Maybe her joy at landing a research position.

"How long ago was that?" Vienna asked.

"About seven years ago. She'd been working at the lab about five when the fire happened." His Adam's apple bobbed. "That night... It was our anniversary. She called to tell me she'd have to stay a little late. To bring her the outfit she'd picked out and she'd change there, then we'd go to dinner. I'd booked a table at Marquette's. That fancy Italian place with the perfect view?"

He paused, as if waiting for Vienna to respond. She nodded. She knew of the place, even though she'd never had a reason to go to a fancy restaurant since she'd moved to Minnesota. His wife had died on their anniversary? How painful.

"Anyway," he continued, "the fire had already started by the time I got there. Smoke billowing into the air, burning and choking. The fire trucks had beat me to the scene. They had the hoses hooked up and everything. It was after work hours so there wasn't anyone else around." He closed his eyes. This had to be so traumatic for him.

"You don't have to tell—" she started, but he held up his hand.

"No, I do have to. I haven't told this to anyone, not all of it." He opened his eyes, and the glossy sheen in them nearly broke her.

She pressed her lips together, then nodded. "Okay."

"She screamed. Brittany. I could hear it coming from somewhere inside. And when I heard her, I rushed for the door, but they wouldn't let me in. They said they were looking for her. That the building had overhead sprinklers, and they'd find her and get her out in time." He shook his head, staring at some fixed point on the table between them. Her chest tightened as she listened. "But they were too late. The sprinklers didn't work in her lab. She'd died of smoke inhalation before they got to her."

Her heart broke for him. "Oh, Hudson, I'm so sorry." She'd heard all about the fire and Brittany's passing, though it had happened nearly a year before she started at the lab. "I didn't know her that well, but she was always a pleasure to work with. We mostly swapped emails, but I had a few video chats with her. She had such a vision for this project and the value we could bring to the world. I remember this one time, when I was especially down about some failed experiments, she said, 'Vienna, maybe this one didn't work, but we are going to find the right formula, and it will change the world.' She had a special way of encouraging others."

A small smile tugged at his lips. "Yes, she did. I was blessed to have the years together that we did. My job kept me traveling often and away from her work events, but I did meet Kevin and Melissa a few times at holiday parties. I'm sorry Kevin's wife has to go through all of this."

"Me, too," she replied. Melissa had always felt more distant to Vienna than Dr. Glickman—maybe because she was more introverted and lacked his warm, friendly manner—but she'd always been polite and gracious. And her faith in Vienna's innocence made Vienna all the more sad that this had happened.

"I know the cops deemed that night an accident," he said, "but now…"

"You're thinking there might be more to it. So am I." What company had Dr. Crofton been about to name? Her mind immediately jumped to Bios PharmaTech. She'd only met the owner, Jared Sherman, a few times, but she'd never cared for his abrupt manner, nor the cutthroat way he ran his company. But then, Bios certainly wasn't their only competition in an unforgiving market.

"What if Brittany was part of this conspiracy?" Hudson's question broke into her thoughts. "What if she was feeding information to whatever competing company is trying to steal from BMRL?" He jammed a hand through his hair. "Maybe I should've dug deeper into her work stuff."

She didn't have the answers, and she couldn't make any promises, but she could offer what she knew. "Brittany was incredibly excited about this project. She shared my vision through and through of finding a solution to a global problem. Of course I can't tell you for sure, but I just can't picture her being involved that way."

He nodded. Stared down at his hands for a minute. "Thanks."

"Is that why you moved out here? To escape the memories of what happened?"

His eyes met hers. "Guilty as charged." Then he stood, letting out a slow sigh, and scooped up his plate. "Done?"

"Let me help." She stood and carried her plate over to the sink after him.

As they cleaned up, he said, "It's always been my go-to habit to turn to work when things are tough. And being out in the wilderness makes God's presence feel more real to me, if that makes sense? When she died, and it seemed so senseless and almost *cruel*, I struggled with my faith for a while. I needed to get away from the constant reminders of what I'd lost, and instead focus on the good things that were left."

"Like work?" She quirked an eyebrow at him. "I know all about that. Guilty, too."

"Really?" He handed her a plate to dry, looking at her with his head tilted to one side. Traces of grief remained in the lines of his face, but his expression had brightened. Like he'd latched on to a mystery to solve.

"Yeah. I… Well…" She paused, suddenly at a loss for words. How did you casually explain to someone that your ex-husband had cheated on you after only a few months of marriage?

"Here." He held out his hand for the last plate she'd dried, then put it back in a cupboard. "Come on out here. I'll crank up the wood-burning stove."

She followed him out to the living room and sat on the sofa, tucking her feet beneath her, while he tinkered with the stove. In a few minutes he had a cheerful fire crackling behind the metal grate, putting out warm, golden heat.

Her shoulders relaxed, and weariness tugged at her limbs. How good it felt to be safe and warm for a bit.

But then he sat down on an opposite chair, one leg crossed over his other knee, waiting expectantly. "You were going to tell me something. What was it?"

She swallowed. Weird how little time they'd known each other, and yet here she was about to spill the story she'd kept hidden from nearly everyone else. "When I was doing my PhD in biochem at MIT, I met a man from another program, Jack Young. He was studying molecular bio, working on a PhD, too, and even though we were in different departments, we had some classes together. He was a few years older than me, very smart and charming. Godly. I looked up to him almost immediately. He seemed to line up perfectly with my vision of an ideal husband.

"Well, when we started dating, I never even considered whether or not this was God's will. Jack and I were both headed the same direction in terms of academics, motivating each other with work, wanting the same things in terms of our spiritual lives. I didn't see all the ways we were different. Or the fact that my imagination had filled in most of the gaps regarding who he really was."

Hudson grimaced, like he knew right where this story was going. "What happened?"

"He proposed when we each had less than two years left in our programs. ABD, as they say—all but dissertation—meaning our coursework was done and now it was a matter of finishing the research and doing the writing. I was thrilled, of course. We set the date and tied the knot about a year later, but almost right afterward he admitted he'd lost interest in his research. Felt like being a scientist wasn't truly his calling, and that maybe God had something else in mind. He wanted to drop out and take a temporary job while he figured things out."

She picked at the hem of her jeans, remembering her utter shock in that moment. How clueless and unobservant she'd felt. "Of course, when you take those vows, you mean them for life." Her gaze met Hudson's, and he nodded. "So it wasn't like I was going to let his career choices interfere with my commitment to him. But it made me wonder how I hadn't noticed, and if there were other things about him I'd misjudged. Anyway, he picked up a job at a nice local restaurant as a waiter and did that for about half a year until I defended my dissertation."

Now for the truly pathetic part of the story. "After my defense, he took me to the restaurant where he worked to celebrate, and this woman, one of his coworkers, came up to wait on our table. And the way they looked at each other..." Her throat closed up. Good grief, it'd been nearly four years. She should be able to talk about this by now without feeling like she'd swallowed a hedgehog.

Hudson waited, watching her, but one hand kept clenching and unclenching. The shadow of her pain reflected back in his eyes, as if he could viscerally feel her grief.

"As you can probably guess," she said, picking up her pace now, rushing through to the end of this awful story, "he told me a few days later he was having an affair with her." Just remembering that moment was like a punch to the stomach. And the way he'd looked at her, with that mixture of pity and happiness about his own escape...

She plowed on, before the memory made her physically ill. "He said he was terribly sorry, that he should never have married me, and he wanted a divorce. I was so flabbergasted I didn't even put up a fight. Just went through the motions and signed the documents and moved on to Maryland to do my postdoc alone. I've been by myself ever since." She shrugged, then tore her eyes away from him before his sympathy made her cry.

Out the big glass window at the front of the cabin, narrow shafts of golden light broke through the trees as the sun slipped downward. Weariness washed over her, sucking away whatever fight she had left. The last twenty-four hours had been nearly the worst of her life, challenging even that day when Jack had finally come clean.

She wanted desperately to believe that God was working all these things together for the good, but it was so very hard sometimes to trust Him.

"I'm so sorry, Vienna. You never deserved to be treated that way." Hudson's gentle tone tugged at her heart, but she couldn't look at him. Not unless she wanted to dissolve into tears. So she mumbled thanks and fiddled with the soft fabric of the hoodie she'd borrowed from him.

Tears pooled in her eyes, anyway, and she made a futile attempt to blink them away before resorting to swiping at her cheeks. It was awful how much an old wound could still hurt, all these years later. And the overwhelming sense of failure.

Hudson rose to his feet and walked over to her. "Come here," he said, then gently tugged her to her feet. She leaned into his warmth as he wrapped his arms around her, cocooning her in strength and security the way he had earlier that afternoon. It'd been a long time since she'd felt this protected. This *not* alone.

"Thank you. For everything." She pulled back slightly to wipe her cheeks, and he loosened his grip but didn't let go. Her heart sped up as she gazed up at him, and somehow a whole host of butterflies had turned loose in her stomach.

His blue eyes searched her face, as if looking for traces of pain to ease. Golden stubble gleamed on his jawline, framing his full mouth.

When those lips curved up on one side, heat burned up her neck and she flicked her gaze back up to his eyes. He'd caught her staring at his mouth. As if she just might want to kiss him.

The thought sent those butterflies into a whirling vortex of confusion. Especially when he leaned closer to her, like he might be thinking the same thing. But before either of them moved any closer, the loud ringing of a phone sent them leaping apart.

Vienna pressed a hand to her pounding heart as Hudson dashed over to the kitchen. Disappointment and relief mingled together in a confusing tangle of emotions. After what she'd just confessed about Jack, about how another man had left her because she wasn't what he wanted, why would Hudson ever be interested in her? Or had she just misread that situation entirely? Maybe he'd only meant to comfort her. Didn't that make more sense? After all, her failed marriage had certainly proven she wasn't a good judge of people's intentions.

"Let me get her," Hudson spoke into the handset, then held it out to her as he hurried across the room. "It's Melissa Glickman," he said.

"Hello, Melissa?" she said into the phone.

"Oh, honey, I'm so relieved to hear your voice," the older woman said. "The police told me what happened at your house. How did you escape from those awful men? And who were they?"

"Hudson rescued me, the same park ranger who helped me last night. We don't know who they were, but we're going to find out. I spoke with Dr. Jeremiah Crofton—he was my old postdoc boss and a friend of your husband's—and he said Kevin suspected a competing company of trying to steal from BMRL. Do you know anything about that?"

Melissa was silent for a moment, then she said, "He never said anything specific, but he did seem more worried in the last several months. Would it help if I look through some of his things?"

"Yes, that could be very helpful." Vienna glanced at Hudson to see if he'd heard. From the way his gaze snapped to hers, he'd caught every word. "How are *you* doing?"

"It's been hard." Melissa paused then made a soft sound that could've been a sniffle. "We're having the funeral on Tuesday. I wish you could be here for it, but until the police get their act together and believe what I keep telling them, there isn't much we can do."

"I wish I could be there, too." Hopefully the rest of BMRL would attend. After all, Dr. Glickman had not only founded the lab, he'd poured his life into it. Yet another reason to make sure Vienna's formula didn't end up with a competing company. "Thank you for your help and support."

She hung up the phone and handed it back to Hudson. "She's going to check through her husband's things to see if she can find anything that might help."

He dragged a hand across his face, suddenly looking as exhausted as she felt. "If you're up for it, I think we should go back to Grand Marais in the morning. I still have a storage unit there, with a lot of Brittany's things." His Adam's apple bobbed. "I...couldn't bring myself to go through all of it before, but we might find something useful."

It was a sound plan, if they could avoid the cops. The

last thing she wanted was to get him into trouble. "Are you sure that's okay? You won't get into trouble?"

He shrugged, his lips tilting into a crooked smile that was somehow both boyish and very masculine at the same time. "Eh, it'll work out. Let me get you a pillow and some blankets. You've earned a good night of sleep."

As she lay curled up under a handful of cozy throws a half hour later, watching the glow of the dying embers, she couldn't help wondering what she'd gotten into.

After Jack had taken her heart and trampled it to bits, she'd thought she'd never even be able to look at another man again. And yet here was Hudson, making her insides do funny flips as he protected her and cared for her. Even these blankets, lightly carrying his scent of cedarwood and sage, brought him continually to the forefront of her mind. The feeling was heady and delightful, like being a teenager with a first crush.

And yet—

She wasn't a teenager anymore. She knew what it felt like to give yourself fully to another person, only to learn too late that you weren't enough for them. That once they'd gotten to know you, they realized you weren't the sort of person they could truly love.

She hadn't been what Jack needed, and she'd been too caught up in her own world to notice that he wanted something—some*one*—else.

Maybe she'd never be the right fit for anyone.

She rolled over, turning her back to the fire and pulling the blankets farther away from her face until the woodsy scent of the stove masked the cedarwood and sage. The whole thing was ridiculous, anyway. Hudson had never asked anything of her, nor would he. He had his own loss to deal with.

Being alone worked well for her. And for him. It was exactly what each of them wanted.

And that's how things were going to stay, no matter how lonely it sounded.

NINE

Hudson flopped over in his bed for the hundredth time. He'd been awake for over thirty-six hours—and chased, knocked out, shot at. Not to mention all the time spent piloting a boat, rescuing Vienna and mulling over the best thing to do next.

He *should* be out cold. He'd fallen asleep just fine. And yet only a few hours later, here he was, lying awake and staring at the ceiling like his bed was the most uncomfortable place on Earth. The time on his clock glowed in red digital numbers, mocking him. 12:07 a.m. Barely after midnight.

Hopefully Vienna was asleep. His brain instantly flitted back to earlier, when she'd shared about that horrible louse of a man who'd married her and then cheated on her right away. She'd fit so neatly into his arms, like she belonged there. And the way she'd looked up at him, like maybe there was something more behind her feelings than a simple need for comfort…

Ugh, this wasn't helping. He jammed a fist into his pillow to fluff it, using more force than truly necessary. They'd just met, for crying out loud. It wasn't like she was looking for a relationship, especially not with everything she'd shared.

And he certainly wasn't looking for anything of the sort, either. He couldn't just let the first pretty woman make him forget Brittany and move on with his life.

He propped up on an elbow to smack his pillow again but then froze.

A scratching sound was coming from outside.

Probably just an animal—after all, Isle Royale was home to plenty of moose, elk, wolves, foxes and smaller critters. But it was better to be safe than sorry.

He lay still, listening. It sounded like it was coming from the window right over his head. Rhythmic and steady, *scratch, scritch, scritch*. A pause, then again.

Too rhythmic to be natural. More like someone working a chisel underneath his window sash.

Adrenaline flooded his system, and it took all his willpower not to spring out of bed. But the last thing he wanted was to let the intruder know they'd been discovered, or else they might shoot. Instead, he slowly eased his body to one side of the bed and then dropped down to a crouch on the floor. He used a few precious seconds to throw on a pair of jeans and a hoodie and shove his feet into boots, then grabbed his gun and cell phone off the nightstand. The chiseling continued at the same steady pace.

Good. They hadn't noticed him moving in the dark. He backed slowly out of the room and into the hall. The rest of the house was silent. Judging by the fact they were trying to break into a back window, he guessed whoever it was didn't want to attract attention. Hopefully that meant they'd go slower. And think twice before shooting.

He tiptoed out into the living room, where the fire in the furnace had burned down to black ash. Vienna's sleeping form was barely visible as a dark mound on the couch. If they could sneak out the front undetected, maybe they could get down to the dock to escape on a boat. Though he'd have to get into the ranger station to get the keys first.

The potential problems swirled in his brain, but he shoved them aside as he crept over to Vienna. First goal was just to get out of the house in one piece.

"Vienna," he whispered, gently shaking her shoulder. "Wake up."

She stirred, rolling over to face him. She blinked groggily and rubbed her eyes before letting them drift shut.

"Vienna," he tried again. "We have to go. Someone's breaking in."

Her eyes flew open, the whites reflecting in the tiny bit of ambient light coming from the kitchen appliances. She shot upright, then fumbled around at her feet until she found her shoes. "What do we do?"

"Shh." He pressed a finger to his lips, then pointed to the door. "Out the front. If we can get to the ranger station, I can take the boat keys." Calling for backup was another option, but not until they could get to a landline again. With no reliable cell service out here, he'd dropped his monthly plan for a pay-as-you-go phone years ago.

A creak echoed from the bedroom, and both he and Vienna froze. Silence reigned for a moment, then Hudson grabbed her hand and tugged her toward the front door. He flipped the lock and eased the wooden door open. Pressing close to the screen, he scanned the path and the woods outside—barely visible in the thin, watery moonlight trickling through the foliage high above.

"Come on," he whispered, easing himself out first and holding the door for her. When she'd slipped past, he latched the door shut, wincing at the soft click. More sounds came from inside the house, a heavy thump followed by lighter ones that sounded like footsteps. It wouldn't take long for them to figure out where he and Vienna had gone. They had seconds at best—not enough time to even start for the path to the ranger station.

He reacted by instinct, grabbing her arm and tugging her in the opposite direction. His cabin was at the far end of the stretch of ranger housing, with nothing beyond except a trail a quarter mile away that led north to Huginnin Cove in one direction or east across the island in the other. Maybe if they could lose their pursuers in the woods, they'd be able to circle back around along the shoreline. Or wait them out until morning, and then find a way to Minnesota.

Brush and low evergreen branches swatted against his legs and face as he pulled Vienna into the forest. There was only a narrow path here—almost an animal run—which served as a shortcut from the rangers' living quarters to the maintained backpacking trail. They'd barely made it into the cover of the trees when the screen door to his cabin flew open, banging lightly against the wood as if the wind had caught it.

"Shh," a male voice hissed. "You want the entire place up in arms?"

"Which way did they go?" came the reply.

At least two of them, then. Maybe more. Vienna's hand tightened around his.

A light flashed on, flickering between the trees like lightning bolts in a thunderstorm. He straightened, leaning backward to use the cover of a nearby trunk, but he didn't dare shift his weight. Not when any sound might alert the men.

"Turn that thing off," one of them hissed. "We split up. Fuller and Watts go that way. Tank and me'll check around the cabin, then go this way. Use your night vision, and don't fire unless you have a killing shot. Otherwise, you'll wake the whole place up for nothing."

Vienna's fingers squeezed harder around his hand, and her palm felt suddenly damp with cold sweat. She'd heard those words, too—*killing shot*. These men had come to kill them.

He could fire off a shot of his own to alert the other rangers to the danger. But most of the rangers out here in Windigo weren't law enforcement—they were college kids looking for a summer of career experience in the outdoors, not an encounter in the dark with cruel gunmen. And the few who had gone to Park Ranger Law Enforcement Academy were all sound asleep. By the time they'd woken up and realized what was happening, the men would be gone. And he and Vienna might very well be dead.

Boots crunched on the main path connecting the cabins as two of the men walked away. A moment of silence followed, then rustling, swishing noises that seemed to fade, as if the other pair had gone around the cabin.

Now was their best chance. He squeezed Vienna's hand and pulled her after him, forcing his feet into slow, careful steps despite the urge to run. But blundering through the woods would draw instant attention, whereas the soft rustling they were making could almost be wildlife. *Lord, please let them think it's an animal.*

When they'd pressed forward for several minutes with no sound of pursuit, Hudson began to think they might make it. Any minute now they'd intersect with the trail leading up from the lake. If the way was clear, he and Vienna could circle back down to take one of the boats. Or at least hide out in the ranger station until the coast looked clear. The men had probably tied off their boat somewhere down there at the edge of the harbor, tucked out of sight of the buildings. With their reluctance to be seen, surely they'd give up before too long.

He picked up their pace, tugging Vienna forward a little faster. But suddenly she stopped, pulling back against his grip. When he turned to look at her, barely visible in the faint moonlight, she had a finger pressed to her lips. He paused, listening. Then he heard it, too—a faint crackling, rustling sound coming up the path behind them.

His heart rate jumped as adrenaline shot through his veins. He had his gun, if it came down to it, but he'd rather not give up their location to the rest of the men if he could avoid it. Could he get a jump on their pursuers? The numbers were against him, but he had the element of surprise. If he could occupy them long enough, Vienna could get to safety.

The gaging station at Washington Creek was less than a mile away. She could hide there until morning. He pulled her close, pressing his mouth near her ear to cover the sound of his voice. "There's a trail up ahead, close by. This path T's into it. You can't miss it. Turn right and follow it until you reach the gaging station at the creek. The gage house is always unlocked. Stay hidden until either I join you or it's morning. Then you can follow the trail back to the lake. Got it?"

She twisted her head, brushing her cheek against his. For a split second he inhaled the soft scent of mint wafting from her hair, wishing they were anywhere but here, with their lives on the line. Then her breath blew against his ear as she said, "What about you?"

"I'm going to make sure they can't follow you." He pressed her close one last time, then released her. *Please God, let this work. Keep her safe.* "Now go."

* * *

The warmth of Hudson's arms lingered in Vienna's mind as she turned away from him. The rustling behind them had grown louder since they'd stopped. There wasn't much time.

She picked her way down the narrow path as quietly as she could, but every step made her feel like an elephant tromping across dry brush. Surely they'd pick up on the reverberations. And Hudson—how could he take on two men at once? But there'd been no time to argue, and she wouldn't be able to contribute anything in a fight. It'd been a solid fifteen years since she'd taken Brazilian jiu-jitsu as a teenager.

Where was the trail? Behind her, Hudson made no sound where she'd left him next to a big tree trunk. What if one of the men slipped past him? Or saw her and fired at her?

She shoved all the unhelpful questions aside and tried to channel her fear into making each footstep as sure and steady as possible. But then sound erupted behind her, a sharp *thwack*, followed by grunts and thumps—Hudson fighting with someone.

A prayer burned her tongue, and she took off quickly. Dodging roots, ducking around low branches—missing a few and getting whacked in the face—anything to stay upright and get as much of a lead as possible. The cold night air raised goose bumps on her skin and frosted the tip of her nose.

What if she missed the trail and got lost? What if Hudson couldn't stop them?

What if they killed him? Fear for him crept into her insides like a fog, chilling her to the bone despite the physical activity.

A minute later her narrow path dumped her into a wider trail—nicely maintained here with mulch and wide enough it was impossible to miss. She froze for a second, trying to remember which direction Hudson had told her to go. Left would lead to the lake, so it had to be right.

She made the turn and opened up her pace into a full run. Her lungs burned in protest, and she wished she'd spent more time exercising over the past few years. Crackling and rustling noises in the woods competed with the thumping of her feet on the trail. If she was this loud, surely anyone still chasing her could hear. And what *were* all those sounds? *Please let them be nocturnal animals, Lord.*

When her thigh muscles ached and her lungs felt like a balloon ready to burst, she slowed her pace to a walk and listened. The sounds of fighting had long since vanished. Far above, a half-moon glowed high overhead, and tiny stars flickered against a black sky. She sucked in great gulps of crisp air, but her heart rate refused to calm down. How far away was the gaging station?

Then she heard it—the sound of running water up ahead. She had to be close. But what was that other sound? More a reverberation she could feel than a noise.

A sinking feeling filled the pit of her stomach as she realized what it was. Footsteps. *Please let it be Hudson,* she prayed.

Forcing her feet into a jog again, she hurried up the path until the station came into view. It could almost have passed as a trailside pit toilet—just a tiny wood-shingled building with a single door on the far side of the creek. A wooden bridge led over the water to it, and a set of stairs led up to the structure, which had been built on a concrete foundation four or five feet above ground level.

The entire area was exposed, with no cover of trees, but there was no sign of movement. She loped up to the bridge and jogged across it, wincing as the boards shifted and strained under her weight. But no gunshot rang out as she went up the steps to the door. It was unlocked, as Hudson had said, and the inside was bare except for some waist-level contraption for measuring the creek's water level, connected to pipes that ran down through the floor.

If anyone happened to come looking, there'd be nowhere to hide in here. And no way out. Her limbs tingled as fresh goose bumps stole across her skin. She needed a weapon. And to know what she was up against. Closing the door behind her, she turned back down the stairs and walked around the base of the station, looking for anything on the ground that might work as a makeshift weapon. A stick or a rock would be nice. Then she spied an old piece of piping tucked against the concrete base behind the station. That would do.

The ground back here was muddy, and the creek levels were high with snowmelt and the rain they'd had the night before. She grabbed the two-foot-long pipe section and considered the ground at her feet. What to do about all these footprints she'd just created? Leaving them here wasn't an option.

She'd just started swiping the end of the pipe through her tracks when she froze. The gurgling of the creek made it almost impossible to hear any other sounds, but she could feel thumps again. She shrunk back against the cold concrete foundation, then dared a peek around the side next to the creek. Her chest tightened. Someone was there, on the bridge. *Two* someones. Their dark forms were clearly visible even in the night.

Which meant—a wave of nausea passed through her—either Hudson had lost the fight, or the other men had caught up with her.

She pulled her head back and rested it against the cold

concrete, listening. Faint footsteps echoed across the bridge, then the soft swish of boots on mulch, low bass notes against the higher-pitched tune of the creek. The wooden steps groaned as someone walked up to the station door and yanked it open.

A light flicked on. She could see it shining out in thin stripes over her head, coming through cracks in the plank walls of the station house. Her fingers tightened on the cold metal pipe, clutching it close to her chest, and she hardly dared to breathe.

The door slammed shut, and the stairs creaked again as they tromped back down. Her heart shot up into her throat, nearly choking her. What if the men checked back here?

Keep going, keep going, keep going. The words ran through her head like a song on endless repeat. Light seared across the ground to her right, illuminating the creek's edge.

Then to her left. She bit her lip, pressing back as far as she could against the concrete foundation. *Please keep going.*

"Come on, nobody's here," a harsh voice whispered, far too close. All the man would have to do was walk forward a few paces and glance around the corner.

She edged closer to the opposite corner, one slow step at a time.

"Lemme just check back here," a man answered.

No!

For a split second her whole body froze. Then she spurred her feet on, sliding around the corner to face the creek a hair's breadth before the light shot across the water next to her.

"See? Nobody," the first one said. "Now, let's get back to the boat and get outta here before they catch us."

"They're not gonna catch us in the middle of the night.

Besides, do *you* want to go back and tell the boss we failed? I don't. We have to keep going."

The light swung away. Vienna released a silent breath, her knees going weak. *Thank You*—

"Wait," the first man said. "What was that? Shine the light back over there."

Her mouth went dry as the light returned, illuminating the ground a few feet away from her. Where a couple of very obvious boot prints stood out in sharp relief against the smooth mud. She hadn't had time to clear them. The flashlight beam stalled on them for a second, then clicked off, descending the world into darkness.

Boots squished on soft mud as the men moved without speaking. They had night vision goggles, didn't they? And tonight, they weren't coming to kidnap her—they were coming to kill.

She lifted the pipe in her hands, raising it like a baseball bat, and edged closer to the corner of the gaging station building. Her fingers clenched so tightly around the cold metal, she couldn't feel them anymore.

She'd only get one chance. And with two of them, her probability of success wasn't looking good. Especially if one came around from the other side. The hairs lifted on her arms, but then a dark mass stepped around the corner next to her, and there was no more time to think or to be scared.

Vienna swung the metal pipe for all she was worth.

TEN

Hudson rushed toward the gaging station as fast as he could, ignoring the pain in his ankle. It was a stupid injury—he'd managed to take out the first man easily with the advantage of surprise, but somehow he'd fallen the wrong way and twisted the ankle while wrestling with the second man. Both attackers were down for the count now, and hopefully wouldn't find a way to escape the makeshift cuffs he'd made using paracord.

But the whole fight—and especially tying them up—had taken far longer than he'd wanted. Now he just needed to get back to Vienna and make sure she was safe.

He was almost there. The trail curved up ahead through the trees and then opened up at Washington Creek, with the gaging station just on the other side of a wooden footbridge. But as he rounded the bend and caught a glimpse of the station house, a woman's cry reached his ears.

Vienna. Not a scream, but more like a groan followed by a series of grunts and thumps. On the opposite side of the creek, he could just make out dark shapes against the lighter concrete backdrop. She was holding her own admirably, whacking at the man with something long and narrow. But a third shape approached from the front of the station house, ready to jump her from behind.

They hadn't noticed Hudson, here on this side of the creek in the shadowy darkness beneath the trees. It'd be tough to get across the creek unnoticed, but even if they did see him, at least that'd distract them from Vienna. There would be no way to shoot, not with her in the mix, so he tucked his gun into his waistband.

His muscles burned with adrenaline as he burst out of the cover of the trees and raced for the bridge. Just as he hit the wood, the man who'd been sneaking up behind Vienna turned his direction.

"Heads up!" he called to his comrade.

Hudson leaped from the bridge, angling for the opposite bank. The man fired off a few shots, splitting the night with sharp cracks made a little quieter with the use of a silencer. The shots bit into the wood where Hudson had been seconds before, splintering the planks.

He landed with one foot on the muddy bank and the other in the stream, deep enough that water gushed into his boot. Pain seared up his leg from his twisted ankle. The man swiveled with his gun, firing again, but Hudson dove for the ground, pulling his boot out of the water with a slurping sound. Then he scrambled forward, lunging for the man's knees and dragging him to the ground.

Mud slathered across his back and arms as he and the man rolled across the ground fighting for the guy's gun. Hudson managed to get a grip on the assailant's arm, then smashed his hand down against a rock half-buried in the bank. The gun popped loose from his grasp. Grunting, the man threw Hudson off and scrambled after the weapon, but Hudson wrapped his arms around the man's waist, stopping him. The attacker's fingers brushed the handle of the gun, but instead of getting a grip on it, the movement sent it slipping down the incline and into the creek.

A few paces away, Vienna screamed, freezing the blood in Hudson's veins. Metal crashed against concrete with an earsplitting clang. Hudson shoved the man away and lunged to his feet, pulling his gun. He slipped and scrambled in his muddy boots toward her. The other man had what looked like a metal pipe in his hand—probably wrestled away from Vienna—and he raised it back to strike as she hunched against the wall, arms over her head.

Stay down, Vienna. He breathed the command like a prayer, then aimed his gun for the man's upper left side where he held the pipe aloft. One breath, then he squeezed the trigger. The man howled, dropping the pipe with a soft *thunk* onto the muddy ground.

He couldn't see in the darkness where he'd hit the man, but the guy was still up on his feet. Still a threat.

"Hudson, look out!" Vienna yelled.

A second later the other man crashed into his back, sending him flying forward. He managed to keep a grip on his gun as he landed face down in the mud. The assailant lunged for it, but Hudson rotated beneath his grasp and landed a punch to the man's face. Vienna was in motion, too, on his other side—he could sense more than see it—and a moment later the metal pipe clanged into something again. Not the hard metallic blow on concrete, but something softer. An answering groan told him she'd just taken out the guy he'd shot at.

"Take that," she said, and his heart swelled. For the moment, she was all right.

He scrambled back from his attacker, raising the gun. "Freeze!" he ordered. "Hands up!"

The man glanced between him and his fallen partner, then lifted his hands over his head, panting heavily.

"Into the station house. Drag your pal along with you,"

Hudson ordered, rising cautiously to his feet. He followed as the man obeyed, slowly climbing the creaking steps. "Vienna, grab that pipe."

Once both men were inside, Hudson took the pipe from her and wedged it through the handle and beneath a vertical pipe running alongside the door frame. It wasn't perfect, but it'd hold long enough.

Hudson walked along the bank again where the fight had occurred, searching the ground for the dropped firearms. The one in the creek bed was too hard to see in the dark, but the other lay on the bank near the station house. He tucked it into his waistband along with his own.

"I guess I knocked it out of his hands with my first swing," Vienna said. Her voice trembled ever so slightly.

He walked over to her, then pulled her into an embrace. She felt real and solid, and he breathed a prayer of gratitude to the Lord for protecting them. "You did good. I'm sorry I didn't get here sooner."

"Thank you for coming. This was never your mess."

"It is now. I told you I would help you, and I meant it." Without thinking, he pressed a kiss to the top of her head. The second his lips touched her soft hair he snapped back to reality. What was he *doing*? Panic lanced through his insides, and he released her abruptly, stuffing his hands into his pockets.

Thankfully she didn't say anything about it. Just glanced around and said, "Do you think there are more of them?"

"I hope not. But maybe," he said. The man he'd locked up was pounding methodically at the back of the door, as if testing it for weaknesses. "It's early season, so the ferry will leave Windigo at 7:30 a.m. sharp for a return trip to Grand Portage. I mean for us to be on it as soon as we can board. I think it's best if we don't take a park service boat.

We want to go incognito." He'd notify the chief ranger as soon as they'd made it safely off the island.

"That makes sense," she agreed. "How do we get from Grand Portage down to Grand Marais, where your storage unit is? Rent a car?"

"Or I'll call an old buddy." Like Sean. Or one of the other old friends he'd neglected over the past two years. He felt bad about it now, but maybe God had put this situation in his life to start tearing those walls he'd built back down. The process was painful, and yet…it felt right. Like it was time to revisit the past and move forward.

She stood watching him, her face bathed in soft moonlight, as she waited for direction. Her implicit trust both warmed and terrified him at the same time. After the way he'd failed to save Brittany, the responsibility felt like too much. But the ranger training in him had grown to be instinctive by now, and he wanted nothing more than to keep Vienna safe.

"Let's follow the creek down to the water," he said. He led the way across the bridge to the opposite bank, keeping near the trees to avoid the squelching mud and slippery rocks closer to the water. "I wish I could offer you a better place to rest, but I think it's best if we avoid Windigo and the harbor until morning. Just in case more of those men are still in the area. How's your arm doing?"

"Stings a little, but it's okay."

His ankle didn't ache as badly now that the boot had taken a plunge into the icy creek water, but he had no doubts he'd feel the effects as soon as they could rest. They trudged on in silence for another half hour until they reached the creek's mouth, where it dumped into a small inlet of the large harbor. To their left, hidden deeper in the trees, the trail ran to a backpacking campsite and on toward Windigo. He led the way to a dry patch of ground tucked in a small grove of aspen trees.

"Now we wait it out," he said, taking a seat on the ground and settling back against a pair of skinny trunks. Vienna glanced around the clearing, rubbing her hands over her arms. Probably cold now that the adrenaline had worn off. It couldn't be more than fifty degrees out here. He patted the ground next to him. "Come here."

She sat, keeping a respectful distance at first, but when he held out his arm she snuggled closer. Funny how strange and yet natural it felt, for her to sit tucked against him like this.

"It's cold," he said, "and you need rest. Get some sleep, okay? I'll keep watch."

"But you need rest, too," she objected, then opened her mouth wide into a huge yawn.

He laughed. "I think one of us might be better qualified for the job of guard than the other."

Her head had already slumped against his shoulder. "Just for a few minutes, then," she mumbled.

When her breathing grew soft and regular, he smiled. Gentle sadness tugged at his heart. Brittany had cuddled next to him like this when they'd watch movies together on the couch—so long ago he'd almost forgotten what it felt like. There was no denying he liked Vienna right here, tucked up against him. And yet…was it wrong? Was he forsaking Brittany's memory by allowing another woman to get this close?

He bit the inside of his cheek. This whole line of thought was nonsense. It wasn't like they were out here cuddling in the woods for fun. He was keeping her warm out of necessity.

In just a few short hours, it would be daybreak. They'd

head for the ferry, get back to Minnesota and hopefully find what they needed to clear her name. He and Vienna could part ways and each go back to their safe, isolated lives. Problem solved.

Then why did this solution make him feel so...*unhappy*?

A bird chirped somewhere nearby, slowly pulling Vienna out of the cozy dream she'd been in—something to do with a fireplace and hot cocoa and the delicious feeling of falling in love. She snuggled in closer to the warmth next to her, fighting to stay in that liminal space between sleep and wakefulness. But then the warm thing shifted, and with a jolt she remembered that it was Hudson she was leaning against.

She jerked upright, heat boiling in her cheeks despite the chilly morning air. The two of them had enough baggage to fill a train car. And the last couple days were far from a cozy dream—more like a nightmare. She needed to keep her distance.

Fresh daylight filtered through the trees, a soft, milky purple tinted with orange-sherbet streaks.

"Hey, sleepyhead." Hudson's voice was husky with exhaustion, and the crooked smile he gave made her toes curl.

No.

This was an intense situation—it only stood to reason they'd have a growing bond after all they'd shared. And yes, he was an objectively attractive man, so why wouldn't she have some butterflies around him? Thankfully logic and reason would always supersede feelings in her book, and she had learned the hard way that she wasn't the type of woman capable of keeping a man's lifelong affection. Some people were just meant to be single.

His blue eyes gleamed in the early morning light, but

she couldn't meet his gaze. Not with all these unruly emotions flittering through her chest. Instead she turned to her shoes, untying, tightening and retying the laces to keep her hands and eyes busy.

"Did you get any rest?" she asked as she worked.

"I may have nodded off for a few minutes." He pulled away from the trees he'd been resting against and checked his own boots. "Never heard any disturbances in the night, so that was good. But we should probably get moving so we don't miss our ride."

He climbed to his feet, and when he offered her a hand, she let him help pull her up. Her hand felt cold when he let go. She followed him out of the clearing as he picked a path through the woods. A few minutes later they popped out onto the same trail she'd taken last night, only heading toward the lakeshore this time. As he walked, he favored one foot slightly.

"You're limping," she pointed out.

He shrugged. "Twisted the ankle last night during one of those fights. Nothing a little rest won't cure. If we ever get any." He turned back and winked at her, making her cheeks flush. Was this what the early days with Jack had felt like? This heady feeling of being on the receiving end of a handsome man's attention?

But remember how that *turned out.* Besides, no doubt she was reading way more into all of this than he ever intended. They'd be parting ways soon enough, anyway.

Relief coursed through her when the harbor came into view fifteen minutes later. Hudson paused, scanning the docks with their smaller boats bobbing against their moorings. A larger passenger ferry that hadn't been there yesterday, with *Voyageur II* painted in black letters on the aluminum hull, was now tied up to one side of the biggest dock.

"I don't see any out-of-place boats," he said. "Either some of them made it back and left, or they anchored in another part of the island and hiked in last night." He pointed at the *Voyageur II*. "That's the ferry. Usually it arrives in the morning and goes around the island, but early season like this, it sometimes docks overnight and returns to the mainland the next day."

A thought made her chest tighten. "I don't have my wallet—it was in my purse at the lab. Did you have time to grab yours?"

He held up his cell phone. "I keep a credit card linked to my phone. Just for emergencies."

"Does this sort of thing happen to you often?" She followed as he led the way along the lakeshore toward the dock.

"Only when I'm with you." He glanced back to flash a crooked grin, and she couldn't help returning his smile.

She kept her eyes on the ground as they approached the dock, half afraid another ranger might stop them. But no one was out on this chilly morning except for the ferry's crew.

Hudson walked right up the gangplank and onto the ferry like they'd already made reservations. A crew member at the top asked for their tickets, and when Hudson said they still needed to pay, she directed him to the appropriate website.

"You can use the ferry's Wi-Fi. Fortunately for you, it's early season," she said. "Otherwise you'd be staying another night." Her gaze lingered on them as Vienna followed Hudson into the passenger area—probably wondering why they had no luggage. The mud caking the hems of Vienna's jeans didn't help.

No other passengers had boarded yet. She and Hudson slid into plastic seats on either side of one of the tables next to a big window. He tapped past his lock screen and made their booking. By the time the ferry's horn sounded and it cast off from the dock, only three other passengers had boarded—a young couple and an older man traveling alone with a backpack.

She breathed a sigh of relief and settled back into her seat as the ferry chugged out of the harbor. Hudson tapped away at his phone for a few more minutes, then looked up at her. "Okay, I've got us a ride lined up in Grand Portage. An old ranger friend who lives in the area is going to loan me a car. I'm also going to email the chief ranger to let him know what went down last night, but I'll wait to send it until we're almost there. Just in case Chief Deputy Nielson is breathing down his neck. We don't want a ride in a police car."

She dozed off during the trip, waking with her head slumped over onto her folded arm on the table. "Ouch," she said, shaking her arm to get some blood back into it and rolling her shoulders.

Hudson chuckled. "Glad you got some rest. Look, we're almost there."

Outside the window, blue water rolled past, but land loomed ahead. Small brown and white buildings dotting the shore marked the harbor of Grand Portage. Not far beyond it lay the border with Canada.

She and Hudson rose from their table and exited the interior compartment through a side door. Wind whipped across her hair. She held on to the deck's metal railing. Spray off the lake misted her hands and face as the ferry turned toward the harbor. Hudson headed for the bow, but as she turned to close the door, she glanced behind them.

A spot of light shone on the water—sunshine reflecting off a boat. She squinted, trying to see what direction it was heading. Definitely toward the harbor. But was it coincidence, or was it following them?

"Hudson," she called. When he turned toward her, she pointed back. "Look."

He walked back, leaning a little over the railing to get a better view. When he glanced back at her, his expression was grim.

"Do you think it's them?" she asked.

"I can't tell from here, but we should assume the worst." He pulled out his cell phone and tapped out a text message, then looked back up at her. "And if they know we're on this ferry, there's a good chance they've arranged a welcoming party."

His phone pinged, and he glanced down at it again. "Good. Mike's going to move the car to the grocery store lot down the block and meet us there. They'll be expecting us to have a ride here, so if we can shake them on foot, we stand a chance at getting away."

As the ferry glided into the harbor, they moved forward onto the deck in the bow. Vienna scanned the dock. A small group of people waited to board the ferry, but no more than a dozen or so this early in the season. The parking lot held several cars, and as she watched, a dark blue sedan pulled out of a spot and left.

"That's Mike," Hudson said, confirming her thoughts. "At least there aren't any police cruisers."

That was something. But the tension still lingered in her chest, especially as she studied the group of passengers waiting to board. Two men lingered off to one side, watching the ferry. As if they were waiting for someone to get off rather than to board themselves. It was hard to see them from this far away, but something about them made her shiver. She grabbed Hudson's arm and pointed. "Look, those men."

His eyes narrowed as he studied them. "They look familiar. In a bad way."

"Yeah."

He ran a hand over his chin, studying the harbor. "The ferry will pull up alongside that dock and run a ramp down from the side. They won't let the incoming passengers on until we all exit. But the only way out is through that turnstile."

She followed the line of his finger as he pointed. The dock jutted out perpendicularly from a concrete walkway that ran the length of this section of the harbor. A tall fence separated the walkway and dock from the parking lot to prevent people from entering without tickets, and the only exit was a tall one-way turnstile a short distance to the left of the dock. Farther down either direction, the fencing ended with the ferry company's property line, turning in toward shore to enclose the parking lot. As the ferry neared the dock, the two men drifted closer to the exit, then stopped and leaned casually against the fence.

"What do we do?" she whispered. As soon as they tried to leave, the men would be there to catch them. "Will they risk chasing us with all these people?" Or was it possible they merely intended to see what car she and Hudson got into?

He clucked his tongue, then shook his head. "I don't know how big of a scene they're willing to make. Where's that boat?"

They walked over to the other side to scan the water.

The boat had continued its course behind the ferry and now bobbed offshore a short distance away. It looked very much like the one that had chased Vienna away from BMRL the other day.

Hudson shot a concerned glance at her and then returned to the front, where the ferry's crew was preparing to tie up the ship as it pulled up alongside the dock. He pulled out his phone, tapped at the screen and held up a picture of a man with dark hair and a friendly smile. "This is Mike. He'll be in the IGA parking lot. It's that way—" he pointed to the right "—inland on the main road, just past a gas station and the entrance for the public marina. He'll have the car keys for you and then he's got another ride coming to pick him up."

Warning bells spiked in her brain. "Why are you telling me this?"

"Because I'm going to create a distraction, and *you* are going to run."

ELEVEN

"No, that's a terrible idea. We can't split up," Vienna objected. She couldn't make a break for it *alone*. "What about you?"

"Get the car from Mike and meet me on the main road as soon as you can get there. Got it?"

She swallowed. "All right. Where do I go?"

"Down the dock to the public marina, then cut up to the street. The IGA is right there."

The ferry drifted to a stop, and the other passengers lined up near her and Hudson as they waited for the crew members to drop the gangplank into place. Hudson squeezed her hand gently, then released it as a crew member unhooked the rope to open the gangplank. "See you soon."

She nodded, every muscle rigid. What did he have in mind?

He let her walk ahead of him, each footstep ringing on the long metal walkway. She reached the bottom and continued up the dock toward the shore. When she glanced back, Hudson had slowed, letting some of the other passengers go first. On the other side of the fence near the parking lot, the two men had given up any pretense of looking casual and now waited right beside the turnstile. One of them looked very much like the man who'd been in charge of abducting her from her house. A chill crept across her shoulders.

Suddenly Hudson cried out behind her, and she turned just in time to see him stumble off the side of the dock and into the water on the other side.

"Man overboard!" a crew member shouted from the ferry.

The other passengers stopped, calling out, "Are you okay?" and, "What happened?" as they stared at the water.

She wanted to watch and make sure he reappeared, but instead she forced her feet into motion, tugging the hood of her sweatshirt up over her head to conceal her face. Running might make her look guilty—as if she'd pushed him, so instead she kept up a fast walk.

An employee came running past from the ticket booth, holding a life ring, and she pointed back toward the lake, calling, "A man fell!" Hudson reappeared at the surface, waving his arms and splashing like he didn't know how to swim.

When she reached the end of the dock, she noticed a thin strand of shoreline running alongside the concrete walkway, not more than a few feet wide and maybe five feet lower. She hadn't dared glance at the men, as she wanted to keep her face hidden, but she'd be even less noticeable down below.

While the splashing and yelling continued down the dock, Vienna dropped down onto the rocky beach and took off, her feet sliding and crunching on loose rock. More yelling—had they noticed her taking off down the beach, like a criminal?

As soon as trees appeared up above on her left, she scrambled back up onto the concrete walk and darted a glance back over her shoulder. Hudson was out of the water now, surrounded by a crowd but easy for her to pick out with a colorful beach towel wrapped around his shoulders.

No one was coming after her, but as she watched, someone pointed her direction. She turned and briskly kept going. A few moments later the trees gave way to the public marina, and she turned to follow a path leading to a parking lot full of trucks and empty boat trailers.

Vienna broke into a jog, running up the marina's entrance road until the back of a large white building came into view on her left. Beyond it, a gas station's large yellow sign gleamed against blue sky. A cramp stabbed her side and her breath came in sharp gasps, but she pushed on at a run until she reached the front of the store, where a red and white IGA sign greeted her.

And there—praise the Lord—was the man Hudson had shown her a picture of, standing next to a blue sedan. He waved as she came into view.

She'd made it. But had Hudson?

"Thank you again," Hudson said, handing back the beach towel to one of the ferry company employees. He'd lingered as long as he could in the waiting area beyond the ticket booth, trying to buy Vienna as much time as possible. But now the passengers bound for Isle Royale were about to board, and he'd lose the protection of the small crowd.

The two men hadn't budged from their place near the turnstile, even though the last of the passengers he and Vienna had traveled with were now filtering past. Any second they'd realize she was gone. Sure enough, as the last person walked past them, they exchanged a glance and began heading toward the ticketing booth and waiting area.

Toward him.

"Well, I'll be on my way," he said to the employee, then

pushed the wrong direction through the waiting passengers toward the entrance.

"Sir," the employee called, "you need to exit that—"

He didn't turn around, and when he reached the turnstile between the ticket booth and the waiting area, he leaped over it, grateful this one was the shorter kind you found in most places. His sore ankle protested at the rough treatment, but as soon as his feet hit the ground, he took off running through the parking lot.

Shouts came from behind him from the two men, but he ignored them as he raced for the road. He burst out onto the main street just as a blue sedan crawled toward him from the right. *Please let it be Vienna.*

Traffic was coming from the left, but footsteps pounded the asphalt behind him. He glanced over his shoulder—one man was chasing. Where was the other? Getting their vehicle. He gritted his teeth, gauging the speed of the oncoming car, then darted across in front of it. The driver honked the horn, slamming on the brakes as his pursuer attempted to follow but then pulled back at the last second.

"Hurry!" Vienna called from the open driver-side window of the blue car.

He practically rolled over the hood and then flung himself into the passenger seat. "Go. Go!"

She punched the gas, making the car's tires squeal as they peeled away. His car door slammed shut on its own, and he yanked the seat belt across his lap, securing it into place. Then he twisted in the seat to see out the rear window. A white van sat at the entrance to the ferry's parking lot. Just as their car rounded a bend, the van tore out onto the main road after them.

"They're after us," he said, turning to Vienna. Both her

hands were on the steering wheel, knuckles white from how hard she gripped it. "We've got to lose them."

A dimple popped in her cheek as she clenched her teeth. "Where?"

He dug backward into his memory, sifting through all the times he'd driven up here. It hadn't been often, at least not on the main highway. But the forest roads—he knew some of those.

"Go as fast as you can," he said, "and up ahead in a few miles, we're going to make a hard right. It's a little single-lane service road the forest rangers use, right after a bend. If we don't miss it, there's a great chance they will."

She nodded, her shoulders rigid.

"You can do this," he said reassuringly. *God, please help us.*

The miles slid past in tense silence as she concentrated on the road. He kept checking over his shoulder. The white van would vanish and then reappear as they wove along the winding road, sometimes gaining, sometimes falling behind.

"Almost there," he said, praying fervently he was right. It'd been *years* since he'd driven this route. If he didn't direct her correctly, they'd fly right past the road. Then there was the possibility that the rangers had started shutting and locking the gate. "When we round this bend, take it as fast as you can, then on the straight, slam the brakes and take a sharp right onto the unmarked road. It's like a driveway."

"Okay." Her knuckles whitened even more on the wheel.

They hit the bend, testing the vehicle's stability limits, but successfully made the corner. And, thank the Lord, his memory was right—there was the service road. "Brake now!" he called, flinging his hand toward the dark strip of pavement barely visible in the woods.

He flung forward against his seat belt as she hit the brakes, then cranked the wheel hard to the right. The car rocked precariously on its side before settling onto four wheels on the narrow service road. Hudson breathed a silent prayer of thanks that the yellow gate was open.

"Pull off to the left, there between the trees," he directed.

She rolled forward, then eased the car off the pavement onto a dirt turnout. Her wide eyes turned to him. "Now what?"

"Now we wait." He swiveled in his seat, facing the rear. The white van had to be close—they should see it any minute. All he could do was pray that they wouldn't notice the blue car wedged into the shadows under the trees.

Vienna shifted beside him. He glanced at her as she pried one hand off the steering wheel, shaking her arm, and then the other. Instead of turning, she watched the side-view mirror.

Hudson mentally ticked off the seconds as they waited in silence. Then suddenly the van flashed into view—a blur of white speeding down the road—and was gone just as quickly.

He let out a slow sigh and turned back around. Beside him, Vienna slumped in her seat.

When her gaze met his, light danced in her eyes. "We did it."

"*You* did it. Great job."

A shy smile flitted across her lips. "We make a good team." She pressed both hands to her chest. "I felt like James Bond for a minute there."

"Well, it's not quite an Aston Martin—" he patted the car's dash "—but it did the job. Let's give them a few minutes head start, and then we'll get going again to Grand Marais."

He offered a silent prayer of thanks. God had been very gracious so far, protecting them every time they'd needed His help. If they could just make it to the storage unit, if they could find what they were looking for—this would all be over.

Just a little longer.

Vienna slouched in the passenger seat, more than happy to let Hudson take over driving, even though her jeans were soaking up some of the water he'd left behind from his dip in the lake. He'd stripped off his soggy sweatshirt and laid it out on the floor in the back seat to dry, and his damp hair stood up at odd angles.

She'd half expected to see the van barreling at them from the other direction, but it looked like they'd actually managed to shake their pursuers for now. "I'm so glad your friend could loan us his car," she said.

"Me, too. Though he might regret that decision after he hears about that van chasing us." Hudson grinned, but then his smile vanished. "I haven't seen Mike in ages."

How long had it been since he'd seen anyone on this side of the lake? And was it hard for him, coming back here?

He shifted in his seat. "Well, if this trip goes the way we want it to, I should be able to return this car to him tonight. Or tomorrow at the latest. Then I'll get to catch up with him."

Tonight. Could it really be over so soon? If Brittany had left information in the storage unit that proved someone was stealing from BMRL or indicated who the buyer was, maybe they *would* be able to go to the police today. Or if Melissa could find something in Dr. Glickman's things that would help clear her name. She hoped and prayed it would be that easy.

And yet she couldn't help noticing a sinking feeling tugging at her insides as the car banked around another curve. Almost like sadness. Hudson's love for the Lord and His creation, his fearless courage and determination to help her, his easygoing nature… She *liked* being with him. A lot.

Maybe a whole lot more than she wanted to admit.

But if things went according to plan, she wouldn't need to see him again. She'd become one of those acquaintances he knew on this side of the lake but never visited.

The thought kept her silent as the warehouse where Hudson had rescued her flashed past. Then her house, where she'd never quite be able to shake his memory. The lab. He'd grown silent, too, and when they passed the sign for BMRL on the main road, his knuckles grew white around the steering wheel.

"When's the last time you were here?" she asked. Her voice felt rusty, the sound suddenly too loud in the small car.

"Yesterday with you?" He said it like it was supposed to be a joke, but the words fell flat. Then he sighed. "Probably too long. Not since I moved to Isle Royale. The estate attorney found a real estate agent to handle selling the house, and I've just kept auto-renewing the storage unit. Friends used to call and email regularly, but the connection isn't great in Isle Royale, and I was so busy with the new job…" His voice trailed off. He kept staring straight ahead out the windshield, not looking her way.

"Sure, that's understandable."

But he shook his head. When he glanced at her, his lips were turned down in a half frown. "Those are just excuses. I could've reached out to them, but I didn't. I didn't want to remember life here, or how happy we were. I didn't want to think about what had been taken from me." He drew in a ragged breath. "As believers we want so much to be able to trust God and understand what He's doing, but I didn't. I still don't know why she had to die."

Vienna balled her hands together in her lap. "I think there are some things we will never understand in this life. I wasn't very happy with the Lord when Jack left me. It didn't make sense that He'd let this man marry me, and then leave me. And now, too. Why let me figure out this formula that could help so many people, and then it gets stolen? I still don't get it."

Hudson reached across the space between them and took one of her hands, squeezing it gently. His touch was warm and comforting, a small gift of grace in circumstances that felt hopelessly difficult. "I think you're right. We're not always going to get it. Maybe someday we'll understand, but maybe not. That's where the faith part comes in." He released her hand, giving her a wry smile. "Doesn't make it easier, though, does it?"

"No. I guess what helps me the most is remembering who God is—that He's good, and faithful, and unchanging, and sovereign, and loving. He's worthy of my trust. And when my faith in Him is strengthened, then I can find peace in the not knowing."

"And who knows?" Hudson said. "Maybe we'll still see the good coming out of this story of yours. We haven't reached the end yet."

"No—" she smiled faintly "—we haven't."

By the time they reached Grand Marais, her stomach was growling. Hudson gave one sidelong glance, snickered and pulled into a fast-food drive-through. They stuffed in a quick lunch of greasy burgers and fries, keeping the conversation light after the morning's heaviness. She laughed as Hudson recounted stories from his early years as a forest ranger, like the time he accidentally flipped a canoe with his boss in it. Or the visitor who chewed him out because the autumn leaves weren't crunchy enough.

She swiped tears from her cheeks and took another sip of her drink. "I'm afraid life in the lab isn't nearly as funny. Though in my grad school lab, we had this little lava lamp I won in a raffle at a vendor show, and any time someone finally got an experiment to work, we'd shut off all the lights in the lab and turn it on to celebrate."

"That's good," he said, grinning. "Did you leave it there, or take it with you when you did your postdoc?"

"I left it. Part of the lab's tradition, you know?" She missed those days. Even though they'd been tainted by what happened with Jack, there had been a lot of good times. She had camaraderie at BMRL now, too, but her focus had shifted—away from relationships and toward meeting goals. Not that achievements were a bad thing, but maybe she'd allowed herself to become a little too emotionally isolated. Laughing with Hudson felt good.

After they'd tossed their trash, he drove them toward the outskirts of town on the west side. Up ahead, rows of storage units with blue garage doors stood behind a chain-link fence. Hudson pulled into the drive and tapped in an access code, any traces of his earlier humor long gone.

He'd told her he hadn't been back here since he'd moved to Isle Royale. This had to be so hard for him. She kept wanting to take his hand, but somehow that felt like the absolute wrong move when they were coming to look through his dead wife's things. At least there'd been no sign of the white van.

After slowly circling past other units, he pulled to a stop in the middle of the third row. Then he climbed out of the car, dug a key from his pocket and unlocked the door. With a loud metal clang, the garage door rolled upward, revealing a dusty assortment of cardboard boxes, framed wall hangings and small pieces of furniture.

"Well," he said, his tone flat, "here we are."

TWELVE

Hudson rubbed his chest as he surveyed the piles of stuff. His heart felt brittle and hollow, like if he pressed too hard it might crumble into more dust coating all these boxes he'd avoided for two years. He'd barely been able to keep himself together when he cleared out the house after the fire—it had taken all his strength just to get Brittany's things boxed up and transported over here. No way could he have sorted it all.

Now the grief felt different, though. Not raw like a fresh wound, but more like the nagging ache of a scar that hadn't quite healed right. Maybe it never would. He'd loved Brittany with every fiber of his being, and maybe he'd always feel her loss.

A warm hand rested on his arm, and he turned to Vienna, suddenly grateful he didn't have to face this moment alone. If anyone could understand his pain, it was her. In fact, she might even have it worse—at least he knew Brittany had loved him, too. Vienna had just been kicked to the curb like an unwanted piece of garbage. The thought stirred a surprising amount of venom in his blood.

"You okay with this?" she said softly.

"Yeah." He said the word automatically, but as he listened to the echo of his own voice, he nodded. He *was* okay. His heart *hadn't* cracked into dust, and it wasn't going to. "It's time. I can't keep avoiding the past forever. Brittany wouldn't have wanted me to, anyway." She would've wanted him to treasure their good memories together and let the rest go.

And she definitely would've wanted him to unearth the truth about what happened to her.

Vienna squeezed his arm, then let go. "Where do we start?"

"Brittany was a meticulous record keeper. She kept file folders with printouts of all her data and even emails. I used to tease her about all the space that stuff took up when a thumb drive is so tiny, but she'd shake her head and tell me she had to have hard copies. Hard copies for everything."

"Sounds about right for a scientist. A lot of the lab work we do isn't conducive to using a laptop. It's a lot easier to keep notebooks and type everything up later. And once you get into the habit of printing stuff out…" Vienna shrugged. "Old habits die hard?"

"So I guess look for anything labeled Office or Desk or Lab Stuff?" He stepped deeper into the unit, scanning the labels he'd written years ago on the boxes in Sharpie. There was a lot here—everything he knew he wouldn't need in his new life on Isle Royale. Kitchen appliances and photo albums, throw pillows with fancy corded edges, Christmas decorations, the china dinnerware painted with tiny flowers they'd received as a wedding gift from Brittany's aunt and uncle… All of it boxed up, waiting for him to pull himself together enough to deal with it. *Sorry, Brit.* He couldn't help feeling like he'd let her down. She would've hated seeing all this stuff just sitting here, going to waste, when *someone* could be using it.

Maybe when this was all over, Vienna could help him sort through it and give some things away. The thought of seeing her again, apart from this intense situation, simultaneously thrilled and terrified him. And then made him feel guilty, because here he was, going through Brittany's things with another woman. One he was undeniably drawn to.

The whole thing was a mess—that's what it was—and he'd be a whole lot better off alone on Isle Royale. Right?

"What about this one?" Vienna's question yanked him out of his uncomfortable thoughts. Only her shoulders and head were visible behind the stacks of boxes where she stood, but she was looking down at something.

He worked his way around a sofa table, taking care not to knock off the lamps and other random decor items sitting on top. Then he stopped next to Vienna, scanning the labels where she pointed.

Brit's Files. "Oh, that does look promising," he said, then moved the upper boxes to get to the bottom two, which bore the same label. "I called her Brit," he added, though that was probably self-explanatory.

"Jack called me Vee."

He grunted as he hoisted one of the heavy boxes of files and carried it toward the entrance, where they'd have more space. "Did you like it?"

She shrugged. "Meh. He said Vienna made him think of sausages."

Hudson broke out laughing, so hard he almost choked. When Vienna scowled, he pressed a hand to his mouth and bit the inside of his cheek. He walked back toward her to get the other box, but first tugged her into a hug. She was stiff as a board at first, then relaxed as he held her close.

"Vienna, your name is beautiful. Just like—" He slammed his mouth shut before "you" popped out. Though, she truly was beautiful, inside and out. No one could argue that point, except maybe her worthless ex-husband. "Just like the city you were named after," he added lamely. "You've seen The *Sound of Music*, right? Hard to get more beautiful than Austria."

Unless it was her.

She pulled back and looked up at him, and the glossy sheen to her brown eyes wrapped electric warmth around his insides. The urge to kiss away that cute little frown on her face swept over him, so forcefully he felt like he'd been hit with a Taser. He jerked his hands back and turned around to scoop up the other box. The last thing he needed to do right now was pour fuel on their already emotionally charged situation. Surely once they'd had some time apart, once he was thinking clearly, he'd see how much better off they were going their separate ways.

"Here," he said, setting the box down near the open door. "We'll be able to see better over here." Using a pocketknife, he cut open the two boxes, then turned to the one in front of him. It was full of manila folders pulled from the filing cabinet they'd kept in their home office. He began pulling the folders out, scanning the titles and flipping through the contents. It felt strange to see Brittany's handwriting again after so long.

"These are all old," he said, shaking his head. "Papers and course notes from grad school classes, it looks like." Why had she saved all this stuff? Maybe she thought she'd need it one day. *Not where you are now, Brit.* That had been his one comfort through all of it—knowing that Brittany had shared his faith, and that she was now hanging out with the One who could answer all her science questions. Thinking about how happy she must be made him smile. "What've you got?"

Vienna lifted a stack of notepads. "Gold. These are her lab books from BMRL. I'm surprised they didn't burn up in the fire. Normally people keep their lab books in the lab."

"She brought them home in the evenings to write up her results." He scratched the stubble on his chin. "Actually, she'd just started doing that, only a few months before she passed."

Vienna didn't respond or even look up. Instead, she hunched over the notepads, flipping them open one at a time to scan the table of contents where each experiment was listed. "There's no reason to think she would've written down her suspicions, if she had any, but these right here—" she tapped the page "—date to the six months leading up to the fire. She was testing a different formula for me, one we thought for sure would work. In fact, the initial results were very promising. It was only after the fire and further testing that we realized it didn't do what we needed it to do."

As she flipped through the notepad, a sheet of paper drifted out. She set the notepad down and picked up the page, then unfolded it. Hudson watched as she scanned the sheet. Then she turned to him, her hand against her throat, and held the paper out. "Read it."

He took the sheet from her.

Lab books were moved again. Not sure if someone is photocopying my data or just looking through it after hours. I'm going to take them home at night. K told me his concerns.

Then a break, where she'd skipped a few lines, and another note. The handwriting here was worse, as if hastily scrawled.

Think I know who it is. Need to confirm first, though. Can't tell this to K without being 100 percent correct. Don't want H to worry, either.

His heart twinged. Here his wife had been dealing with all of this at work, and she'd never mentioned a thing. "H" had to be him. Who was "K"? Dr. Glickman?

He dragged a hand over his face and handed the sheet back to Vienna, who tucked it into the notebook and set it back on the stack. "She must've figured out who it was. Maybe even confronted them." Vienna nodded. "And they started the fire to silence her."

She'd been targeted by that fire. Murdered. All because she'd wanted to do the right thing. His heart ached for Brittany. What thoughts had run through her head? Had she been afraid? Relieved to know she'd be with her Savior soon?

His stomach hurt. And the way Vienna was watching him, her dark eyes so thoughtful and full of compassion, wasn't helping. He felt painfully vulnerable, like she could see his beating heart right there beneath his ribs. "I'm so sorry, Hudson," she said, her voice hoarse. Her eyes gleamed with moisture.

At her grief for *him*, something cracked inside. He pulled her into his arms, tucking her against his chest where her head fit perfectly beneath his chin. They stood that way for a long moment.

"You okay?" she whispered, looking up at him. Creases lined her forehead, and he traced a thumb across her skin to smooth them away. When he glanced down to her mouth, so close to his, it felt like the most natural thing in the world to lower his face until his lips met hers.

For one glorious second everything was right in the world, and then she pulled back. "Hudson, I… I'm sorry." She pressed her fingers to her lips. "I never should have— The case, and Brittany—"

Right. Of course. Kissing Vienna was the *last* thing he

was supposed to be doing right now. He backed away from her, busying his hands picking up notebooks and setting them down again.

"At least *she* wasn't the bad guy," he said, forcing out words. That was his only consolation. But whoever was, was still out there. He gritted his teeth. "Do you think K means Kevin Glickman?"

"That's my best guess. And H…" She frowned.

"Me. I know. Thanks, Vienna. It's a relief to figure out what may have happened." He tucked the flaps back into the box at his feet and brushed off his hands, wishing he could brush away all the painful memories so easily. And yet, it felt right to finally know what had happened. "Are you good with taking this to the police? They'll be able to keep you safe from those men, and with this evidence, they'll reopen the investigation of the fire. Since you weren't at BMRL back then, it shouldn't take them long to realize you're being framed."

She pressed her lips together but nodded. "I think it's time. I've put you in danger long enough. Here, we should take these with us." She held out a stack of lab notebooks. "These are all the ones with her experiments for BMRL A15—the formula we thought was going to work. I put the note back in where I found it."

"Hold on to those for a sec while I put these boxes back." He closed her boxes back up, then carried them back into the unit. Whoever they assigned to the case would probably want to search in here again. That thought would have horrified him a few days ago, but now it felt right. Like Brittany would be vindicated, and he'd finally reach some closure on this chapter of his life. He'd always feel her loss, but for the first time, he felt like maybe, just maybe, he'd be able to move on.

Vienna's beautiful smile greeted him as he replaced the boxes and walked back toward her. After all this was over, and she was free…would she want to see him ever again? She'd been hurt, too, but was there a chance she also wanted to move on? Open herself to new possibilities? Had that kiss meant anything to her? A foreign sense of hope and excitement fluttered beneath his ribs.

Should he say something to her about it now?

Before he could make up his mind, his cell phone rang. He dug it out of his pocket and glanced at the caller. Melissa Glickman. That's right, they'd given her both his landline and cell number. She must've tried him at home first.

"It's Melissa," he said, holding the phone out to Vienna.

She connected the call and said, "Hey, Melissa, what's up?"

He couldn't hear what the other woman was saying, but the way the blood drained from Vienna's face was unmistakable.

Something awful had happened.

"Slow down," Vienna said, struggling to process Melissa's words through the woman's sobs. Hudson was watching her, his expression pinched with worry. "You found *what* in your husband's files?"

Melissa sniffled, then made rustling sounds like she was wiping her face. "I'm so sorry, Vienna. I just… I never thought…" She paused, as if collecting herself, then went on. "I found a file folder of printouts. All these email exchanges between Kevin and Jared Sherman."

Jared Sherman. "I knew it!" Vienna snapped. "I never trusted him or that company. But why was Dr. Glickman in contact with him?"

"There's no easy way to say this. Kevin offered to sell

him your formula. And it wasn't the first time, Vienna. These emails go back for at least two years." Melissa's words dropped like a bomb, blasting apart everything Vienna thought she knew about her employer.

Bios, had beaten them out on more than one grant in recent years. Was that why? Because *Kevin Glickman* had stolen from his own company? All along she'd believed his concerns that someone was stealing, but could it have been him this whole time?

She shook her head. No, that couldn't have happened. "But Kevin founded BMRL. Why would he steal from his own company?"

"He didn't want to tell anyone—" Melissa sucked in a sobbing breath "—but BMRL is on the brink of going under. I found other papers in here—bad credit reports, loan rejections, payments to a bankruptcy lawyer. He sunk almost all our savings into the lab without telling me. I think he saw this as the only way out."

"But, my research," Vienna objected, as if she could argue her way into undoing all the bad things that had happened. "We would've been able to get a grant for sure." None of it made sense. She *knew* Dr. Glickman. He was a good man. And yet…was it possible he'd been driven to that level of desperation?

The older woman sighed. "It was too late. He'd already made the deal. I wish he would've talked to us about it. Not done this." She broke down into tears again.

"I'm sorry, Melissa." Why had Dr. Glickman chosen this course of action, instead of asking for help? Surely if he'd spoken up, they could've done something. Figured out some solution. Anything but this. And now he wasn't even alive anymore to learn from his mistakes. But it was just so impossibly hard to believe. She chewed the inside of her cheek. "Why did they kill him? The men who broke into BMRL shot him right away and came after me. If he was behind the deal, why did Sherman have him killed?"

"I don't know. A double cross?" Melissa said. "A way to get the formula and keep the money?"

Whatever the reason, there was a silver lining. This evidence would surely be enough to clear her name, especially when combined with what she and Hudson had found. And yet Brittany had said she needed to be 100% sure before approaching Kevin. Had she figured out the truth too late? And then he panicked and started the lab fire to kill her? Though it was awful to consider, it could be the missing piece of the puzzle.

"We need to get this evidence to the police," she said into the phone. "Can you meet us at the station?"

Hudson had been watching her with rapt attention, and at her words, he dug his keys out of his pocket and walked out of the storage unit, Brittany's files tucked under one arm. Maybe this whole dreadful situation was almost over.

She followed him out as Melissa answered, "I'm on my way to the lab. Can you meet me there instead? I'm bringing the files from home, but I want to check his records at work. The police were so focused on you as the suspect they might have missed something. They blocked off most of the building for the crime scene, but the front offices are still accessible through the main entrance."

Hudson pulled the metal rolling door shut and locked the unit.

"Yes, we can be there in twenty-five minutes," Vienna said. "We'll notify the police so they can meet us also."

"Already done." Melissa paused, and when she spoke again, Vienna could hear the smile behind her words. "Vienna, I'm sorry you had to go through all of this. I hate that

Kevin was involved in this way, but it makes me feel so much better knowing at least your name will be cleared."

"Thanks." She clicked off the call. Then she took a deep breath and handed the phone back to Hudson. "She wants us to meet her at BMRL. I'll explain everything on the way."

"Should I text Sean, my friend on the force?" he asked as he opened the passenger-side door for her.

"If you want to." She pulled the door shut and waited until he slid into the driver's seat. "Melissa already asked the cops to meet us there."

"They'll probably send Chief Deputy Nielson again." He made a face, and she laughed. It only took him a minute to tap out a text. Surely his friend would make sure the police came.

Her heart felt lighter than it had in days, since before that terrible moment the armed man broke into her meeting with Dr. Glickman. Maybe they'd find justice for Brittany and the lab, and for the attack on Dr. Crofton. She still didn't know if he was dead or alive. The thought hurt.

As the car wound its way up the coastline toward the lab, she went over everything Melissa had told her with Hudson. Repeating the evidence against Kevin Glickman didn't make it any easier to believe. Maybe she could accept the idea of him being desperate enough to steal, but *murder*? From the grim set to his jaw, Hudson, too, was struggling to understand what had happened. And yet, the promise of this disastrous case being over was dangling right in front of them.

"So if we can pin this on Jared Sherman and his hired goons," he said, "your name will be cleared. And this whole thing will be over."

"Yeah, it looks that way."

A crooked smile formed on his lips. "Sounds like a huge

answer to a prayer. Maybe God is going to give you a happy ending after all?"

She grinned back. "Maybe so."

His blue gaze glanced at her, filling her insides with warmth. Would that happy ending involve seeing him again? As she surveyed the rugged line of his jaw, the easy yet determined set to his shoulders, there was no question in her mind what answer *she* wanted to that question. Maybe it was reckless, putting her heart on the line again, but it was hard to argue against all these feelings swirling through her system. She'd only known him a few days, and yet he'd protected her, cared for her, put his life on the line for her again and again. Who wouldn't want to spend more time with a man so giving, kind and honorable? Not to mention attractive, strong, smart…

A little sigh escaped her lips, and she clamped them shut, warmth burning in her cheeks. Her thoughts were running out of control—after all, Hudson had never said he shared any of these wild feelings. If anything, he'd shared about how much he was still grieving his wife's death. Yes, they'd kissed, but had that meant anything to him? Or had he merely been caught up in the moment?

"You okay?" he asked, darting a glance at her.

She pressed cool fingers to her flaming cheeks, hoping he wouldn't notice the red. "Uh, yeah. Fine." When her voice squeaked, she cleared her throat. The thought hit her that now *would* be a perfect opportunity to tell him how she felt. Or, at least a little part of it. Or even ask him what his plans were, something safe and noncommittal. But as she met those clear blue eyes studying her, the thoughtful way he was taking her in, she panicked. Pluck her feathers and stick her in a roasting pan, because she was a chicken.

What if he rejected her? Maybe he wouldn't right now—

maybe he was too polite, and he'd play along for a while—but then he'd still reject her later when he realized he didn't feel the same way. Wasn't that what Jack had done? She'd never thought she'd pressed him into the relationship, but had she?

Maybe she was just the type of person meant to be single. Maybe no one would want to stick with her. Especially not a man as amazing as Hudson.

He glanced from the road back to her again, his lips parted slightly. Like there was something he wanted to say, or he was waiting to hear the right thing from her. The air felt heavy and charged at the same time, though she couldn't understand why. It had to be all in her own head.

She forced out words, anything to deflate the tension. "Just eager to get this mess cleaned up and move on with my life."

The look on his face vanished like early morning mist on the lake—like she'd only imagined it—and he nodded as he turned back to the road. "I hear you. Very understandable."

Disappointment wreathed through her insides, thwarting the sense of safety she'd wanted by retreating. *This* was why she loved science. Experiments either worked or they didn't. The numbers might not add up to the answer you expected, but they still added, the same way every time. There was none of this ambiguous and confusing emotion.

But instead of feeling better when the brick and glass building of BMRL came into view through the trees ahead, her stomach twisted. Once these freshly traumatic memories faded, would it be her place of refuge once more? She didn't know a whole lot about the structure of the company, but maybe there'd be a way to pull it back from the brink of bankruptcy. With Sherman in jail and Bios PharmaTech off their tail, maybe they'd be able to find investors to back the lab until they could get a government grant.

Hudson had faith God could bring about a happy ending. She sucked in a slow breath and offered a silent prayer as he pulled into the parking lot. *Please, Lord, work all things out to the good.*

The lot was empty except for a lone silver Audi parked near the front. It was late now, after working hours, though in the wake of Dr. Glickman's death no one would be here except for crime scene investigators.

"Your friend has a nice car," Hudson said, nodding toward the brand-new looking Audi as he pulled into a spot a few over.

Melissa did, considering what she'd just told Vienna about Kevin dumping their savings into BMRL. Maybe that car payment was just another burden that had weighed him down until he couldn't see any other way out.

Wind rustled the trees as they got out of the car. When Vienna closed the car door, the slam echoed across the empty parking lot like a gunshot. A chill tiptoed down her arms, raising goose bumps. Must be nerves getting to her, now that they were so close to the end. But from the way Hudson checked his gun and re-holstered it, she wasn't alone in the feeling.

As they headed up the sidewalk toward the front door, Hudson stopped. He scanned the parking lot again. "Did you hear that?" he asked softly.

She hugged her arms across her chest. There was nothing out here but their two vehicles. "No. What was it?"

He shook his head. "I don't know. Something just feels… off. Too quiet, maybe. And it seems like the police would be here by now."

"Melissa will know." She gestured toward the door.

"We'll have to text her to let us in. The front door will be locked."

But when they reached the glass entrance doors, one of them was propped ajar by a rubber door stopper. That was definitely against protocol—but then Melissa wasn't an employee. Or a cop protecting a crime scene. Maybe she just hadn't thought about it. Vienna reached for the door handle, but Hudson stopped her.

"Wait," he said. "Something's rubbing me the wrong way about this. I'd feel better if we scout the perimeter first."

The door was so close, and inside, Melissa had the files she needed to clear her name and pinpoint the true culprit. Yet she trusted Hudson, and if his gut said something was up, she'd wait a little longer.

"Okay." She followed close behind as he walked back down the sidewalk the way they'd come. Nothing moved in the parking lot, and the surrounding woods were quiet. At the corner of the building, they turned to follow a sidewalk that led down to the storage area and mechanicals beneath the big deck in the back, and beyond it, the docks. In the distance, boat engines hummed out on the lake, and waves lapped gently on the rocky shore, but there was no sign of anyone else on the property.

A crease formed between Hudson's brows as he scanned the area, then turned to her. "Sorry, I don't know what I was expecting to find. It looks clear."

She laid a hand gently on his arm. "It's better to be cautious. I appreciate that."

"Thanks." His lips tilted, but the worried look stayed in his eyes. "We might as well walk the whole way around to check the other side."

They followed the sidewalk down to a covered path running beneath the edge of the deck. A chill breeze off the lake made her shiver. The sun was slipping down in the west on the other side of the building, casting long shadows on this side. Surely Melissa was wondering where they were by now.

They reached the far corner, and Hudson paused once more to scan the forest that ran along the side of the BMRL property, but there was nothing out of place.

He dragged a hand through his hair, already ruffled by the breeze. "Clear. Guess my hunch was wrong." A troubled expression lingered on his brow, but he rounded the corner and led the way uphill toward the front of the building and the parking lot.

When they reached the front door, he held it open for her. "Between Brittany's files and whatever Melissa found, we're going to get your name cleared. This will all be over soon."

That thought brought a measure of peace as she stepped inside the dark front lobby. Why hadn't Melissa turned on the lights?

Suddenly, a hand clamped over her mouth and wiry arms hoisted her off the ground. As the sickly sweet smell of diethyl ether enveloped her senses, she registered a loud *thunk*, followed by grunts, coming from somewhere behind her. The glass door fell shut, rattling like it might break.

Before blackness took her, one last horrifying thought formed in her brain:

We've been found.

THIRTEEN

Vienna blinked away the bleariness in her eyes as the space around her resolved into a room. One she knew very well, in fact—her own lab. Except everything was upside down...

The man carrying her like a sack of potatoes dropped her ungraciously onto the floor, and she crumpled into a heap on the hard linoleum. Horrible ether, still clouding her senses. She shook her head, trying to clear her mind. If she could only think clearly, maybe she could figure out what was going on. Find Hudson. Get out of here. And where was Melissa?

"Tie her up," a man ordered.

As hands reached for her, her gaze landed on a pipette tip lying close by on the floor, nearly invisible with its clear plastic. Hardly a weapon, but better than nothing. Her fingers just managed to snatch it up as the man lifted her. He hoisted her into a seat, then proceeded to lash both wrists to the armrests of her desk chair with thin rope. How fitting that things should end here, where it had all started with Dr. Glickman's death.

Please protect us. Help us, Lord. He had a plan, even in all of this, to bring about good. *Whatever it is, I trust You.*

Melissa sat nearby, strapped into another chair. Duct

tape covered her mouth, and tears mingled with dark mascara streaked her cheeks. A pile of manila folders and loose papers lay scattered over the floor, as if Melissa had been startled by the intruders and dropped them. Yellow police tape barricaded off the area near Vienna's desk. There was no sign of Hudson—only three men wearing ski masks and carrying weapons.

What had they done with him? What if they'd...*killed* him? Knots formed beneath her ribs, twisting up her insides until she couldn't breathe.

"Where's Hudson?" The words came out slurred as her body fought to shake off the effects of the ether.

One of the men laughed, making fire flare in her stomach. How *dare* they? And was this all Bios PharmaTech's doing?

"The ranger? You don't need to worry about him." He moved over to Melissa, pulling out a switchblade and flipping it open. The older woman's green eyes went as wide as dinner plates.

"No!" Vienna shrieked. "Don't hurt her!"

"She's not your concern anymore," the man snapped. He cut loose enough of the ropes to haul Melissa to her feet. She shook her head frantically, screaming behind the duct tape covering her mouth. He passed her off to one of the other men, who dragged her out the door and into the hall.

They weren't going to kill her, were they? Vienna's mouth went dry, and she swallowed. "Where are you taking her?"

"That's the boss's concern, not yours."

The boss... He had to mean the owner of Bios PharmaTech. The police were coming—could she stall these men long enough with questions?

"So who's your boss? Jared Sherman?" she asked.

A low, grating rumble came from one of the men as he laughed. "That's funny, real funny."

"I know he's behind all of this," she went on. "I know Kevin Glickman arranged to sell my work to Bios PharmaTech, and for some reason you had him killed, anyway. Why *did* you kill him? So you wouldn't have to pay him?"

The men exchanged a glance. She wished she could see their faces. None of them appeared injured, so they weren't the same ones who'd abducted her the other day. At least, not all the same.

"Time to take care of this one?" one of them asked, waving his gun at her.

The man with the knife glanced at his wristwatch. "We've got a few more minutes."

For *what*?

Regardless, her job was to stall for time. "You didn't answer my question," she pressed. "If you're going to kill me anyway, you might as well tell me. Why did you kill Kevin Glickman?"

The man with the knife pocketed his blade, grabbed a lab stool and pulled it up, then tugged the ski mask off of his head. She grimaced—it was the same man who'd forced her to enter her laptop password.

"Nice to see you again, sweetheart." His fake smile curdled her insides. "I hate to break it to you, but Kevin wasn't the mastermind behind this plan. You got the buyer right— Jared Sherman from Bios PharmaTech. But he's not the one who hired us or set any of this up. He's just footing the bill through his payments for the formula. Half up front, half on delivery. But we can't deliver with this many loose ends. Hence—" he waved his hand in the air "—all of this."

"What are you telling me? Kevin is innocent?" she demanded. "Melissa found the emails."

"She must not have mentioned the ones between him and his close friend and colleague, your former mentor."

Vienna's brows pinched together as confusion raked her insides. "Jeremiah Crofton? But, he was killed, too. I saw it on the Zoom call."

"You mean you *think* you saw it," the man said. "Crofton lives in Maryland. Didn't you wonder how we could get men over there so swiftly?"

"Well, yes—"

"Easy. There were no men in Maryland because Jeremiah is *right here*. That little fake death scene was entirely for your benefit. But since he'll be here to witness your death any minute, you might as well hear the truth."

What? Dr. Crofton was in on this whole thing, too? But—

"I don't understand. Why did he kill Kevin Glickman and steal the formula? If they were partners, Kevin would've given it to him. *I* would've given it to him if he'd asked." In fact, she *had* given him all the data. And why wouldn't she? The whole project had been his idea in the first place. He never needed to steal it.

The man lifted his hand and rubbed his fingers against his thumb. "Money, baby. It's all about the cash. Why share the payout from Jared Sherman if you don't have to?"

Her brain raced to catch up. Dr. Glickman had lost his life over a poor deal—and all this time since, Jeremiah Crofton had been working to acquire her data, then lure her out of hiding so he could take her out, too. Her thoughts snagged on something the man had said moments before. "Did you say he's here? As in *here* here, at the lab?"

"Any minute now." The man glanced at his wristwatch. "Shooting you would be far easier, but he wants to make sure it's done right. Looks like an accident and all."

But if Jeremiah Crofton was heading here, to the lab, and Hudson hadn't been able to escape yet—

Her chest tightened. They would kill Hudson, too, if they hadn't already.

Hudson struggled against the ropes cutting off circulation to his hands, grunting in frustration. The tape across his mouth crinkled and tugged at his skin. Hard concrete dug into his back where they'd dropped him on the sidewalk outside the building.

"Knock it off." A hard kick rammed into his back, punctuating the man's words.

He'd done his best to fight off the man who'd jumped him from inside the building, but he'd been totally caught off guard. He gritted his teeth as another wave of anger washed through him. How could he have been so stupid? But there'd been no sign of anyone else here.

Until now, of course. Now they'd pulled the white van right up into the parking lot next to his car. Were they going to drive off with him? Kill him and dump the body somewhere? And what had they done with Vienna?

The thought of her tied up—or worse—made him twist his wrists harder. But the only result was the cords digging into his skin even tighter, with his ankles bound also and an armed man kicking him whenever he moved too much. Where were the police? He strained to hear sirens in the distance, but the only sounds were the rustling of leaves on the trees and the occasional boat engine on the lake.

Footsteps echoed on the concrete sidewalk as more men appeared around the corner of the building, from the path leading up from the lake. Where had they come from? One of the boat engines he'd heard?

"Get him up. You can remove the tape. He might have something interesting to say."

Hudson strained to see who was speaking against the bright backdrop of the sky. An older man with a graying goatee and short, thinning hair. He was lean and fit, as if he worked out. Who was he? The buyer Melissa had told Vienna about?

Two of the men—their faces covered with black ski masks—hauled him to his feet. The one who'd attacked him ripped the tape off his face, and then they dragged him toward the door. Following behind, the older man kept a gun pointed at Hudson's back. An escape attempt now would be a death wish, but maybe he'd be able to figure something out once they were inside.

"Who are *you*?" Hudson asked, craning his neck to see over his shoulder.

"The same thing I was going to ask you," the man replied. By now they'd reached the front door, and he held it open. "I'm an old friend of Vienna's. And Kevin Glickman. Dr. Jeremiah Crofton. I'd offer to shake hands, but…" He smirked as the men dragged Hudson past and into an empty lobby.

Dr. Crofton? Hudson frowned. "You're Vienna's boss from her postdoc. But she saw you die."

Crofton chuckled as he led the way down a hall. "It *was* an Oscar-worthy performance, I must say. You must be that ranger she picked up along the way." His lip curled as he turned to survey Hudson, like he was stepping around a stray dog. "It's a shame you got tangled up with her, but it can't be helped now."

"The cops will be here any minute." Hudson scanned the hallways as they proceeded deeper into the building, looking for anything that might help their situation. The doors were closed, the lights off in the rooms they passed. There was no sign of Melissa. Were they holding her with Vienna?

"Then it's a good thing we're on schedule." Crofton pointed ahead to where light streamed out of an open door. "Take him inside. I'll be back in a moment."

Even though Hudson knew Vienna would be in here, his insides still crumpled at the sight of her tied up in a chair, three armed men pointing guns at her. Now they had six men—no, seven, counting Crofton—to deal with, and neither of them was armed.

Her expression fell as their gazes connected. Utter disappointment. He couldn't hold it against her—she'd been counting on him to protect her, and he'd let her down. The sense of failure burned deep, a visceral reminder of the last woman he'd failed, and suddenly it was hard to stand under the weight of shame. If by some miracle they made it out of here alive, there was no way he could tell Vienna how much he cared about her. Not when he couldn't even manage to keep her safe. She deserved a man who could protect her.

He sucked in a deep breath and forced his spine to straighten. Now wasn't the time to give up, or to dwell on his mistakes. There'd be plenty of time for that later. Right now, he needed to figure out a way to get them out of here. He might be able to knock down one of the guards and get a gun, but it was a long shot, especially with his hands and ankles tied.

Before he could decide on the best move, Crofton reappeared in the doorway. Vienna inhaled sharply. "How could you do this?" she asked, her eyes narrowed.

He gave her a wide grin. "Vienna! You always were one of my favorite postdoctoral researchers. I'm truly sorry it had to end this way. If Kevin had just cooperated…" He held up his hands and shrugged, as if none of this was his fault. "Anyway, too late now."

Crofton walked past Vienna and gathered something off the floor—lab benches blocked Hudson's view. When he stood, he had a stack of file folders. Then he nodded to the men near Vienna. "It's time."

They moved away to a cardboard box Hudson hadn't noticed before sitting on one of the counters.

"Better tie the ranger to a chair," Crofton added as he headed for the door.

As the two men dragged him toward a nearby stool, Hudson strained to see what the others were doing. Carrying something—and shaking it over the floor, it looked like. Then one came closer to him, and both the sudden, pungent fumes and distinctive white bottle with a red cap left him in no doubt of what they were pouring over the room.

Lighter fluid.

FOURTEEN

Vienna wrinkled her nose as the smell of lighter fluid permeated the room. She wished she could flip on the vent hood fan or put on a mask. But toxic fumes were going to be the least of their problems soon.

Her heart broke for Hudson as she helplessly watched the men tie his ankles to a stool. He never should've been in this position. He should still be back on Isle Royale, helping stranded boaters and giving directions to backpackers, not in the hands of these men. It was all her fault. Somehow she'd become a magnet for trouble, and the smartest thing he could do was to stay away from her. That would be the first thing she'd tell him, if she ever got the chance.

She'd been working at the cords around her left wrist with the pipette tip this entire time, whenever the men weren't looking. Not only was it painfully slow, but she'd gouged herself with the tip at least once or twice. Of course, a little blood wouldn't matter if they were burned to a crisp.

Suddenly Hudson moved, flinging the stool out from beneath himself and kicking it into one of the men. They'd only managed to tie one leg. He balanced on the other, but as the stool crashed into the man, both of them fell to the ground. The other guard slammed the butt of his gun toward Hudson's head, but he managed to slide out of the way just in time.

"Leave him!" Crofton ordered. "We need to get out of here."

The man who'd fallen scrambled to his feet and kicked Hudson in the stomach. Vienna winced at his groan. Then the two men headed for the door, where Crofton waited. She pried away at the cords as she watched them walk.

Suddenly the knot gave way, and her wrist was free. She ripped her arm away from the armrest and fumbled to untie the other, wedging the pipette tip into the knot to loosen it. The men vanished into the hallway, except for one who had his back to the inside of the room.

Wriggling her fingers beneath the cord, she loosened it enough to yank her other arm out. But her feet were still tied, and there wasn't time to unravel more knots. Especially when the man turned back into the lab with a box of matches. She shifted her hips forward in the chair, setting it rolling just enough to reach the nearest lab bench, where a glass beaker gleamed in the overhead lights.

The man struck the match.

She snatched up the beaker and cracked it onto the black benchtop, shattering it into pieces.

"Hey!" the man yelled at her.

"Just light it!" Crofton called from behind him.

He tossed the match onto the ground, close to the wooden cabinets supporting the bench between her and Hudson. The flames shot up instantly as the lighter fluid caught fire. She slashed at the bindings around her ankles, heedless of the glass cutting into her palm.

The cords fell away. Choking smoke exploded into the air as flames licked up the cabinets. Why weren't the overhead sprinklers turning on?

Vienna jumped out of the chair, sending it rolling away from her, and raced around the growing fire to get to Hudson. The door to the room slammed shut.

She slid to her knees next to him, coughing as smoke bit into her eyes and lungs. He'd managed to contort himself around to get his hands next to the leg that was tied, where his fingers worked at the knots.

She pushed his hands aside, then sawed at the rope until the frayed edges gave way. As she worked on his wrists, the doorknob to the room rattled. Like someone was locking the door. Her palms grew slick, and she nearly lost her grip on the glass.

Hudson pulled away from her. "That's good enough. We've got to get out of here." With a sharp twist of his arms, he snapped the partially cut ropes apart. Keeping low to avoid the choking smoke, he rushed to the door, twisted the knob and yanked it open.

The man on the other side hadn't succeeded in locking it yet. When Hudson tugged unexpectedly, he flew into the room with the door. Hudson tackled him to the ground. "Go!" he yelled to Vienna.

Behind her, glass shattered as a shelf full of beakers splintered apart. She lunged past Hudson, stumbling out into the hall. Sirens wailed outside the building, and footsteps hammered the linoleum hall. Jeremiah Crofton and his thugs were running away.

Hudson had succeeded in subduing the man left to lock the door. He shoved the man's gun into his waist and hauled him to his feet. "Come on!" he called to her. "Cops are here."

"But Jeremiah is getting away." Holding her breath, she leaned back inside the room to shut the door in an attempt to slow the spread of the fire. The entire building had a top-of-the-line fire response system—it should be going off by now, putting out the fire. Had they tampered with it? The cinderblock walls would slow the spread between rooms—unless the ceiling tiles ignited. She prayed it wouldn't come to that.

Smoke issued out from beneath the closed door, rising over their heads and spreading out into the hall.

"Come on," Hudson urged. He waved her forward, and she led the way through the darkened corridor as he hauled the man after him.

The sirens were louder now—hopefully just out in the parking lot. Maybe they'd even be able to intercept Jeremiah. And what about Melissa? Had the men killed her? Or was she still inside somewhere, alive?

"Did you see where they took Melissa?" Vienna asked over her shoulder as she raced toward the front entrance.

"No, I never saw her," Hudson called back.

That didn't bode well. Where could she be? What if she was still trapped inside somewhere, alive but unable to escape?

Red and blue lights flashed in the parking lot outside the front door. The sight should have eased the band around Vienna's chest, but she couldn't shake the feeling Melissa was in danger.

Then she heard it, so faint she wasn't sure whether it was real or her imagination—a woman's voice calling her name.

"Do you hear that?" she asked as she shoved the front door open for Hudson.

"What?" he yelled over the noise of the sirens. Maybe it *was* her imagination.

At the sight of the cop cars and fire truck, the man Hudson had captured suddenly threw his weight sideways, trying to break loose. Across the parking lot, police officers shouted and came running.

"Vienna!" There it was, louder again—someone calling for her from inside. Melissa?

She bit her lip, glancing between Hudson, the man wrestling with him and the officers on their way. It would only take a second to check, and she might save Melissa's life.

Slipping back inside, she let the glass door fall shut. "Melissa? Is that you?" she yelled, hands cupped around her mouth. It was so hard to hear over the sirens, but easier with the door closed.

"Help! Vienna!"

Her heart leaped. Melissa *was* still inside. She jogged back into the main hallway, looking both directions. "Where are you?" she yelled.

"Here! In the closet!" Pounding accompanied Melissa's words, coming from the hall to the left.

Vienna turned in the direction of the sound. The fire must be spreading—a choking mist of smoke rippled over her head, making her cough. She reached the closet where the pounding was coming from and yanked the door open. Melissa was inside, surrounded by mops, brooms and buckets. She'd managed to get the duct tape off her mouth and her hands untied, as evidenced by the scraps on the floor, but apparently the closet door was locked. Streaks of mascara lined her cheeks.

"Oh, honey," she sobbed, falling into Vienna's arms. "I didn't think anyone would find me. That awful man locked me in here. They were going to leave me to die. Thank you for coming back for me."

She hugged the distraught woman, then rotated to brace an arm around her back for support. "Of course. But we need to get out of here."

She took a step forward, but Melissa stayed rooted to the ground. When Vienna turned, her brows pulled together, something hard and circular pressed into her side.

A gun.

Hudson wrestled the man to the ground, jamming his knee into the man's chest. Officers were running toward him, and the parking lot seemed filled to the brim with emergency vehicles and flashing lights.

Just like the night Brittany died. The thought crashed into him like a ton of bricks. Heat burned across his skin, swiftly replaced by soul-deep, numbing cold that made him shiver.

Apparently sensing his distraction, the man shifted beneath him, rolling sideways like a slippery eel. Hudson flung himself at the man, this time flipping him over and securing his hands behind his back. "You're not getting away," he said.

The man's chest rumbled as he laughed. "Neither is she."

Hudson frowned. "What do you mean?"

No answer. But the man's gaze darted to the door behind them.

At that moment, a pair of officers arrived. Hudson eased off the man's back as one of the cops clapped a set of cuffs around his wrists. He climbed to his feet and turned back to Vienna.

Then froze. Where was she?

She'd been right behind him coming out the door. Had she gone to speak to the officers?

Somewhere around the back of the building, glass shattered. A faint trace of black smoke drifted up, marring the blue sky. He whipped his head back toward the fire trucks. Why were they just sitting there, doing nothing? Didn't they know the building was on fire? Or had the entire alarm system been deactivated?

Now that he thought about it, not only had the overhead sprinklers stayed off, but there also hadn't been emergency lighting or an alarm, either. Maybe they *didn't* know about the fire.

"Hey," he yelled, pointing toward the building. "There's a fire inside one of the labs! In the back!"

Firefighters in tan suits striped with neon yellow leaped into action, grabbing gear and tugging long hoses off the truck. The two police officers hauled the man away to one of the cars. But what about Crofton and the other men? Did anyone know where they'd gone? And what about the van?

He wanted to run in six directions at once, but the most immediate concern was finding Vienna. When he scanned the chaotic parking lot, she was nowhere to be seen. Neither was Melissa. Had the two women been taken to one of the ambulances? Or—

Vienna had asked about Melissa as they exited the building. Had she gone back inside? Was that what the man had meant? That she hadn't come out?

A pit formed in his stomach, as the night of Brittany's death played out in his mind. The parking lot a hive of chaos, just like it was right now. Choking smoke filling the sky as firefighters scrambled to get into position. Uniformed officers barricading the door. Her scream splitting the night and ripping apart his heart.

That time he'd arrived too late. But this time… This time no one was blocking the door. And if there was any chance he could save Vienna, he'd gladly give his life to do it.

Then a sound reached his ears over the noise outside, high-pitched but short, like a scream cut off—coming from inside the building. *Vienna*. The pit in his stomach threatened to swallow him whole.

Before anyone could restrain him, he raced back to the door, barely noticing the pain in his sore ankle. And praying he wouldn't be too late.

"Do it again and I shoot," Melissa growled into Vienna's ear. "Got it?"

Vienna nodded, blinking away the moisture forming in her eyes. Melissa released her hand from Vienna's mouth.

"I don't…understand," she stammered. Why was Melissa threatening her?

"Yes, thank you for coming back." Any trace of fear or crying had vanished, and Melissa's face settled into a scowl. Her green eyes had hardened into glittering emeralds. "Otherwise, you might have lived to testify against Jeremiah and Jared. But not now." She smiled sweetly. "Now you'll just be another tragic victim in an accidental lab fire."

"It was *you*, wasn't it? Never Dr. Glickman." Suddenly it all made sense. How the men had entered BMRL using an access card instead of forced entry. How they'd known about her meeting with Dr. Glickman and where she lived. How they'd been able to disarm the fire sprinkler system. Melissa had been feeding them information all along. "I *knew* he wouldn't have made a deal to sell my formula."

"No, all Kevin would do was keep pouring our cash into that sinking ship of a lab until we went down with it, just like the *Titanic*." Melissa laughed bitterly. "I had to take matters into my own hands."

"Hudson knows the truth," Vienna said defiantly. "He'll tell the police what happened."

Melissa tilted her head to one side and clucked her tongue. "Not if he never gets the chance. You, of all people, should know how fast things can change. Besides, he'll never know *I* was involved." She latched a wiry hand around Vienna's arm, her expensive acrylic nails digging into her skin through the thick fabric of the hoodie. "Now, your turn to die. Give my regards to Kevin."

She yanked Vienna's arm, twisting her toward the closet. The gun dug into her side. More smoke was pouring into the hall, drifting lower now and making it harder to see and breathe. But she'd seen the lights on the fire trucks—the firefighters would be here any second.

Could she elbow the gun away from her side and escape? Would she be fast enough? Before she could move, Melissa shoved her unexpectedly from behind, sending her stumbling into the closet. The door slammed shut, leaving her in suffocating pitch darkness. She spun, hands fumbling for the door lever.

Something heavy banged against the other side, and when her fingers finally clasped the cool metal of the lever, it wouldn't move. Not like it was locked, but like Melissa had wedged it into place with something on the other side.

Footsteps thumped away from the closet. Vienna called for help and pounded on the wooden door, first with flat palms, then, when her sliced-up hand objected, by banging her shoulder against it. The door shook in its frame but didn't budge.

She was trapped, and Hudson had no idea that Melissa was responsible.

FIFTEEN

"Vienna!" Hudson called as he sprinted through the entry and skidded to a stop in the hallway. The smoke was getting worse out here now as the fire spread unchecked deeper inside the building, making it hard to see. His eyes burned. He coughed and pulled his hoodie up over his mouth and nose. "Vienna!"

His breath caught as a figure emerged from the smoke to his left. Vienna?

No—the stature was too short for Vienna, the body type not the same. He jogged up to her. The woman had both hands pressed to her face, covering her mouth, and her eyes were rimmed with red. Her brown hair was streaked with gray, and she wore a pantsuit and heels. His subconscious made the connection first.

"Melissa Glickman?" he asked, cocking his head to one side. He hadn't seen her in years, not since that last Christmas party before Brittany passed.

"Oh, thank goodness." She pressed a hand to her chest, and her knees wobbled like she might go down. Hudson offered his arm to brace her upright. "Those men locked me in a closet, and I just now managed to get out."

"Have you seen Vienna?" He glanced down the hallway in the direction she'd come, but the smoke made it hard to see.

Melissa shook her head, then leaned against him as she nearly doubled over coughing. "I haven't seen anyone."

"But I heard her scream." At least, he *thought* he'd heard a scream. Had it been only an overactive, stressed imagination?

"Maybe you heard me? I was calling for help."

He chewed the inside of his cheek. *Maybe.* But then he heard noises coming from down the hall. Thumps. And, as he strained to listen, a woman's voice yelling.

Melissa coughed again, shuffling her feet.

"Shh," he said. "I thought I heard—"

"Please get me out of here," Melissa whimpered, pulling him toward the entryway. "I feel like I'm about to collapse."

Outside, the voices of firefighters yelling to each other carried through the front doors. They were focused on rigging up the hoses to fight the fire from the back, but someone was bound to come in here soon. Maybe if he just led her back to the entryway, she could call for help.

A muffled scream sounded again, much more distinct this time, along with pounding, as if someone were hitting a door.

"It's got to be Vienna," he said. "Just head that way and—"

"I was afraid you'd say that." Melissa went rigid for a split second, then she shoved back from him. Something flashed in her hand.

He barely had time to register what the object was before a deafening crack sounded. His ears were ringing, and his left leg stung like a giant wasp had gotten him. She'd *shot* him.

Instinct took over, and he lunged for Melissa, tackling

her to the ground. The gun slid out of her grasp and clattered to the floor. She rolled over to grab for it, but Hudson had the size advantage and shoved her away.

He scrambled across the floor, snatching up the gun. Something wet and slick coated his hands and his leg throbbed, but he swiveled onto his bottom and raised the weapon. Smoke issued from the corridor leading to Vienna's lab, making it hard to breathe even down here near the floor. How much longer did they have before it was too much?

Melissa pulled up onto her feet, her face twisted into a vicious snarl.

"Freeze!" he yelled. *Please give up.* He didn't want to shoot her, even if she was culpable in this mess.

Footsteps pounded in the corridor behind Melissa. A second later gleaming headlamps appeared, shooting rays of light through the swirling smoke like the special effects in a theater production.

Melissa turned toward them, her hands lifted in…supplication? "Help!" she called. "He's shooting at me!"

What? Red-hot anger seared Hudson's insides. "Melissa Glickman, you are under arrest!" he managed before he broke off coughing. Firefighters appeared on either side of Melissa and took her arms. Another approached Hudson. "*She* shot me," he said, pointing at his leg. "Look."

"Drop the gun, sir," he said, his voice echoing through the breathing mask he wore.

Hudson held up the weapon, then turned it to face the handle toward the firefighter. The man took the weapon and tucked it into his belt.

"The closet," Hudson said, pointing in the direction of the thumps. "There's a woman trapped inside." He pressed sticky, wet hands to the floor and forced himself to his feet. His left leg objected, nearly giving out beneath him, but he managed to shift his weight to the right before he went down.

"You're injured," the firefighter said.

"Later. Come on." Hudson hobbled toward the closet, dragging the annoyingly weak leg behind him.

"Let me get you out—"

"No!" He forced his way down the hall, blinking back the tears forming in his stinging eyes. The acrid smell of smoke permeated his sinuses. Through the haze a door came into view, something red and tube-shaped wedged against the door lever—a fire extinguisher.

The firefighter beat him to the door and worked the extinguisher free, then pulled the door open. Vienna stood on the other side, blinking wide-eyed in the light of the man's headlamp.

Praise the Lord.

"Vienna!" He stepped toward her, accidentally putting his weight on the bad leg. Pain shot up into his torso, so intense he grunted and crumpled to the ground. Blackness edged into his vision, sweeping away the smoke, the firefighter's piercing headlamp and Vienna's stricken face.

"Hudson!" His name ripped from Vienna's lips as she watched him go down. Hearing that gunshot had been one of the worst moments of her life, and now, to see him lying prone on the floor like this… It was sheer agony.

How could she have ever thought she could walk out of his life and never see him again? Everything she'd gone through with Jack—all the disappointment and hurt and loss—paled in comparison to the terror of the possibility of Hudson dying.

Please God, save him. Otherwise he'd never know how

much he meant to her. How much she cared. Even if he didn't feel the same way, he deserved to know.

The firefighter stooped down and wrapped his arms beneath Hudson's shoulders. "We've got to get him out. No time to wait for help."

"Okay." She pressed cold fingers to her face, as if the pressure might hold back the sob building in her chest.

He started to move, dragging Hudson's feet, then paused. "You okay to walk?"

"Yes, I can walk." Vienna kept pace next to the man, glancing frequently at Hudson to see if he'd recovered. The thin trail of red streaking from his left shoe made her chest go tight. Melissa must've shot him. How much blood had he lost already?

A rush of fresh air hit her as she pushed the glass front door open and held it for the firefighter. She sucked in a deep breath that ended with her chest hitching into a sob. The firefighter heaved Hudson outside and away from the building, then called across the parking lot, "Medic! We need a medic over here, stat!"

She crouched near Hudson's side, holding one hand. His skin was still warm, and a pulse still flickered in his wrist. "Hudson," she whispered softly. "Don't leave me."

His eyelids fluttered open. "Hey." He squeezed her hand, then winced when he tried to move.

"Stay with me," she said, her vision blurring.

"I'm not…going anywhere." His half smile tugged at her heart.

She tried to smile through her tears. He was a mess. The pants on his left leg were stained with wet blood, his face was battered and his clothes were covered in dark soot. Still, he was the most handsome, wonderful man she'd ever seen. Inside and out.

Where were the medics?

EMTs were scurrying across the parking lot with a stretcher. Not far away, an officer had handcuffed Melissa and was stowing her in the back seat of a police cruiser. Shouts from behind the building told her the firefighters were still working to put the fire out. Thankfully labs like this one were designed to slow the spread of fire between rooms. They'd have to wait and see how bad the damage was.

She pulled back, giving the EMTs space to load him onto the stretcher. As she watched, a police officer appeared by her side.

"Are you Vienna Clayton?" he asked. When she nodded, he showed her his badge. "Chief Deputy Nielson. Good to finally make your acquaintance, Ms. Clayton."

"It's *Dr.* Clayton, actually."

The two EMTs hoisted up the stretcher and started for the ambulance. Without her. She'd have to stay here and deal with the cops. Maybe even be taken into custody. She might not see Hudson again for a long time.

Her lip quivered despite her best intentions not to cry. "Am I under arrest?"

"Not anymore, ma'am." Nielson glanced toward the police cruisers. Melissa's head was visible in one. Near another, two more men were being placed into the back. They must have been captured while trying to escape. She didn't see Jeremiah, but he must be there, already tucked into one of the cars.

Relief gushed through her system like water breaking through a dam, so intense she thought she might collapse.

"Here," Nielson said, taking her arm. "You'd better get checked out, too, Dr. Clayton." He guided her toward the same ambulance where the EMTs were loading the stretcher carrying Hudson. When her gaze drifted back to where her assailants were being held, Nielson said, "We caught them around back, trying to escape in a boat. We'll need your testimony, of course, but with what we've seen here, there's no grounds to take you in."

When they reached the ambulance, she shook his hand. "Thank you, Chief Deputy Nielson."

He touched the brim of his hat and headed back toward the police cruisers.

She climbed inside and buckled into a seat near Hudson's head in the front of the ambulance. One of the EMTs, a young woman with black hair, sat on the side, working swiftly to press gauze to Hudson's wound and check his vitals. The other closed the back doors and latched them.

Suddenly, with a squeal of tires, the ambulance shot forward. Far too soon for the other EMT to be driving. Alarm spiked through her system, and she glanced at the woman taking Hudson's blood pressure. Her eyes had gone wide.

Through the back windows, the other EMT was clearly visible running after the ambulance, his arms waving.

"Hey!" Vienna called, turning in her seat. A small window over her shoulder allowed her to see through into the cab, where the top of a man's head was just visible. She banged her uninjured palm against the glass. "Slow down! What are you doing?"

But as the man pulled the vehicle out onto the main road heading north—away from the hospital—he spun around to laugh at her. It was Jeremiah Crofton.

She froze, every cell in her body going into full paralysis. Somehow he'd evaded the cops and managed to steal the ambulance, with her and Hudson trapped inside.

"Let us out!" she yelled, pounding the glass again. "You know this will never work. They'll still catch you!"

In response, Jeremiah slammed the accelerator, jerking her back against her seat. The EMT had abandoned the blood pressure cuff and now clutched the bars under her seat with white-knuckled hands.

On the stretcher, Hudson groaned. "What's going on?"

Vienna leaned forward, placed her hands on his temples and kissed his forehead. "You just rest. We're going to be fine." *Right, Lord?* She gritted her teeth. He had a plan, even now.

"Doesn't sound like it," he grunted. "Tell me what's happening."

She swallowed. It'd be better for his health to keep him in the dark, but with Jeremiah's maniacal driving, there was no way to keep it secret. "Jeremiah Crofton's behind the wheel."

He groaned again. "Why won't that guy give up?"

"I don't know. He's taking us north."

"Canada?"

"They'd never let him across the border." She sucked on her lip. They'd be to Grand Portage soon. What was he planning? To kill them, abandon the vehicle in some remote place and then cross the border alone? Unless Melissa or one of their hired guns had given him up, the police still didn't know he was involved. Was he banking on being able to escape?

"Where are you taking us?" she yelled over her shoulder.

No response. But now red and blue police lights flashed in the distance on the road behind them, visible through the back windows.

"The cops are chasing," she told Hudson, since he couldn't see the road.

The ambulance's speed increased, rocking dangerously

as it took corners far too fast on the twisty coastal road. Jeremiah must have noticed the chasing cruisers.

"Give up, Jeremiah!" she called to him through the window to the front. "Nobody needs to get hurt."

"If you think I'm going to jail, you don't know me very well," he growled. "And if I go down, you're going down with me. It's too late to run now." His words brought back her years working for him in the lab as a postdoc—his stubborn determination and brusque, forthright manner that intimidated too many undergrads. She'd seen it as a strength at the time. Now…

She squeezed her hands together into a tight ball.

"What do we do?" the EMT asked, panic lacing her tone. Vienna studied her for the first time, noticing the woman's dewy-smooth dark skin and hair tucked into a ponytail. She couldn't be more than a few years out of college. "What if they can't catch up? Should we jump?"

Vienna shook her head. "Not at this speed. And I'm not leaving Hudson. How's his leg?"

The woman's throat bobbed, and she tore her eyes away from the police cruisers to look back down at her patient. The thick wad of gauze she'd taped to his leg had red stains creeping through, but not nearly as alarming as it had been at the lab.

"It hurts," Hudson grunted. "Great time to be in a car chase," he said wryly.

She glanced over her shoulder again, scanning the road ahead. If there were any county officers up here in Grand Portage, maybe they'd be able to set up a roadblock. But as she watched, Crofton suddenly veered away from the main road, flying off the asphalt onto a gravel driveway without slowing. The ambulance fishtailed, and Hudson groaned in discomfort.

"Where's he going?" he asked as the vehicle bounced over washboard ruts at a painful pace. "I thought County Road 61 was bad enough."

From the dredges of her memory, an image flashed into her mind from one of the first boating trips she'd taken with the Glickmans after moving out here. She jerked upright. "I know where he's going."

Her throat tightened, and she swallowed. "There's a cliff on Lake Superior, just before you round the headland into the bay for Grand Portage." The soaring, black rocks had captured her imagination back then, enough that she'd snapped several pictures on her phone. Never did she think she'd be in a vehicle hurtling toward the edge of them.

She glanced between Hudson and the EMT. "We have to get out of this ambulance."

Every fiber of Hudson's body ached, his leg most of all. Lying here on this stretcher, his adrenaline slowly ebbing away, had made the throbbing pain all the more noticeable.

But at Vienna's words, a new jolt flooded through his system. His muscles went taut and the pain receded into a pesky nuisance.

"How much time?" he asked. If he tilted his chin far enough back, he could just see her—an upside-down version of her, anyway.

She had her back to him, watching out the front window. "I know where we're going. I don't know how long this drive is. I've only seen the cliff from the lake. But the trees look like they're getting thinner up ahead. Minutes, at most?"

The poor EMT gasped, covering her mouth with a hand. His heart went out to her—she didn't deserve to be in this position. A click sounded behind him, and he whipped his head around, straining to see. Vienna rose and twisted in her seat.

"What are you doing?" he demanded.

She studied the window between her and the cab. "If I can open this thing, maybe I can crawl through and—"

"That's a terrible idea." *Because it's likely to end in you getting killed.* His fingers fumbled for the straps binding his body to the stretcher, then he worked the buckles loose. "This thing's got wheels, doesn't it?"

He caught the EMT's eyes, and she nodded.

"Then we're going out the back." He forced his aching body into an upright position.

Vienna pulled away from the window and slid closer to him. "What do you have in mind?"

"He's going to slow when he sees the cliff—it's human nature to fear death—and then if he commits, he'll slam the accelerator. Maybe attempt to jump at the last second out the side door. Well, we're gonna bail as soon as he slows."

Hudson slid toward the end of the stretcher, working his way toward the doors at the back. "You two get on the stretcher. I'll open the doors as soon as he slows and give you a push."

"What about you?" Vienna's voice had gone an octave higher.

"I'll jump on the back. Okay?" Or at least he'd try. He might end up jumping and rolling instead. What mattered, though, was saving the two women.

"Hudson, let me," Vienna said. She and the EMT unlocked the stretcher from the floor and released the wheels, allowing it to raise up. "I'll get the door. You won't be fast enough." She turned to the EMT. "Get on behind him. Like a toboggan."

He opened his mouth to argue, but the vehicle had

started to slow. Both he and Vienna glanced backward. Blue water beneath bluer sky filled the space in front of the ambulance, with only a short expanse of green. It was now or never.

"Do it," he commanded, tightening a buckle across his lap. "Now."

Vienna reached forward and popped the lever. The left door flew open.

"Hey!" Crofton yelled from the cab. His angry face appeared for a second in the window before his foot slammed on the accelerator.

The forward momentum sent the stretcher flying toward the doors. Vienna just managed to throw the other door open and fling herself up onto the stretcher behind the EMT as they sailed out.

For a split second they hung in midair like a sled going off a ramp, then the stretcher slammed down onto the ground. It careened over the rough ground, nearly toppling before Vienna jumped off the back and managed to slow it to a stop.

In front of them, the ambulance sailed over the edge of the cliff. Hudson's gaze met Vienna's, her eyes wide, and they both turned to stare at the empty space where the vehicle had been. A screeching, splashing noise followed. Vienna jogged over to the edge to look as he turned to the EMT.

"You okay?" he asked, scanning the woman for injuries.

Her jaw was slack, eyes as large as dinner plates, but she nodded. He loosened the buckle around his waist, twisted his body until his legs dangled off the side and managed to slide his feet to the ground.

Before he'd made much progress toward Vienna, she

came jogging back, a frown across her lovely features. Sirens blared behind them—the police cruisers had caught up.

"Show me," he said, nodding toward the cliff edge. She didn't argue. Instead, she draped one of his arms around her shoulders and helped him hobble to the edge.

Down below, waves crashed onto large rocks, where the ambulance had become a twisted pile of red and white metal half submerged in the lake. The driver's door was still closed. Crofton hadn't tried to bail.

"It's over," she breathed, looking up at him. Her dark eyes glistened in the fading sunlight, and he thought she'd never looked more beautiful than she did at that moment.

A smile crested his lips. He rested a palm against her cheek, then leaned toward her, pressing his mouth to hers. Joy and exhilaration flooded his insides as he pulled away and saw the same emotions flitting across her face.

"I love you," he said simply. No preamble. No fancy speeches. But those things had never been his way.

Her mouth hitched at the corners. "I love you back."

He stared into her gorgeous brown eyes. "I didn't think I could feel this way about anyone again after Brittany. But when you were trapped inside that building, and I didn't think I'd get to you in time… I knew I loved you."

Her expression sobered. "I've never been so scared as when I heard that gunshot and knew you were out there with Melissa, where I couldn't warn you. After everything that happened with Jack, I'd resolved to let you go and not tell you how much I care, but—" She clamped her mouth shut and shook her head, her dark eyes glistening. "That would've been lying. Because the truth is, I'd go through anything for you."

"Anything?" He raised an eyebrow. "Like a nighttime

chase through the forest? Or a burning building? Or an ambulance about to go over a cliff?"

"Or putting myself out there and admitting how much I love you, Hudson Lawrence."

"I guess the Lord did work all that out for the good, didn't He?" He squeezed his arm around her shoulders. "But we shouldn't be surprised."

She went up on tiptoe, leaning her face toward his, and he kissed her again.

The sound of boots crunching on grass made them both turn to see a police officer approaching. "Sorry for the, er, interruption. Are you both all right?"

He glanced toward Hudson's leg, where the gauze had adhered itself to his exposed skin. The bullet would need to be surgically removed, and depending on the damage to his muscle, there might be physical therapy. There'd be the case to work through with Vienna and the police. The storage unit to clear. Decisions about the future. But for now, in this beautiful moment with her, all of that could wait just a little longer.

He hugged her close and smiled at the officer, feeling his answer down to the marrow of his bones. "Never better."

EPILOGUE

Eight months later

Vienna's breath puffed white and hung in the air as she wrapped gloved hands around the frozen railing of BMRL's newly rebuilt deck. Lake Superior's waves tossed frothy white on the black rocks below as a light wind nipped at her cheeks. It was cold out here, but good. Behind her, soft light glowed from the windows. Sunset came terribly early this time of year in December, but even the early darkness did nothing to dampen her spirits.

A door opened behind her, and she turned.

Hudson strolled out in a thick black parka, hands buried deep in the recesses of his pockets and a lopsided grin on his face. "Thought I might find you out here."

"Hudson?" she squealed, then clapped a gloved hand to her mouth. "I'm so glad you made it."

"I wouldn't have missed it for anything." He walked over and drew her into his arms, then kissed her. All thoughts of what was to come fled her mind at his familiar touch and firm, protective embrace. When he released her, he tapped her nose lightly with a finger. "Your nose is turning red. You ready?"

She smiled, the smallest hint of her joy welling up inside.

In only fifteen minutes, she'd take the podium inside the large new conference room—capable of holding a hundred people—to accept her role as the director of research and commemorate the reopening of the facility. "Yeah. God is good, isn't He?"

As Hudson studied her face, his eyes sparkled. "You're really beautiful, you know that?"

"Even with my frozen nose?" She crinkled it and made a funny face.

"Even then." He kissed the tip of her nose. "Especially when those wheels are cranking in your mind." He glanced at the building, then back to her. "They're blessed to have you."

She thought back to last spring, and the long months of untangling the mess Melissa Glickman and Jeremiah Crofton had created. Melissa had gone to jail on several charges, including murder, and Jared Sherman had been convicted of theft. After sharing her formula with the scientific community, Vienna had secured a partnership with a major drug company to begin the long manufacturing and clinical trials process. It would still take years, but her new antibiotic would be making a difference around the world soon. And between the insurance money and a large government grant, BMRL had been rebuilt and would have the funding it needed to continue research and development for years to come.

God had been very good.

She blinked back the liquid forming in her eyes as she stepped closer to him. He held out his arms and tucked her against his chest, and his soft scent of sage and cedarwood cocooned her in warmth. After recovering from the injury to his leg, he'd had to go back to Isle Royale for the season, and their prolific digital correspondence, along with a handful of weekend visits, had only made her more and more convinced that Hudson was exactly who she thought he was—dependable, loving, invested in her. His love was sacrificial and steady—much like the love of God. And her love for him... Well, she'd fallen head over heels. Now that his commitments for the year were done, she couldn't help hoping there might be more for them on the horizon.

"Thank you, for helping me make all of this happen," she said as she pulled away. "I could never have gotten here without you." She wouldn't be *alive* without him.

He pressed a soft kiss to her forehead. "Vienna, I'm so proud of you. I know how hard you worked to make this happen. And to get your antibiotic into the hands of people who can share it globally." The dancing light in his blue eyes settled into something deeper that pulled at her heart. "You are a remarkable woman, and I..."

His gaze shifted to the building and then back to her face. A crooked grin formed on his lips. "I have a question to ask you."

Her heart rate tripled in the span of a microsecond, shooting like a rocket to the moon as he dug into his pocket and dropped down onto one knee. When he pulled his hand back out, a diamond ring glistened between his fingers.

"Vienna Clayton, will you marry me?"

She pressed both hands to her mouth, and this time there was no holding back the tears springing into the corners of her eyes. "Yes, of course! But—" She broke off. Frowned. A long-distance relationship was one thing, but how were they going to make a long-distance *marriage* work?

He rose to his feet, still holding the ring, and smoothed a thumb across her crinkled forehead. "You don't want to email me every night to say good night from over here?" Laughter danced in his eyes, along with some secret he'd been holding back. "I'm taking back my old job as a forest ranger in Superior National Forest. They've got a spot for me as soon as I want it. Which is—" he glanced at an invisible wristwatch tucked beneath his parka "—about eight months ago. From the moment I met you."

She laughed and flung her arms around his neck. He twirled her in a circle, then set her back on her feet. "Are you sure you won't mind giving it up?"

"What, my isolated little cabin where I hid all alone?" He held up the ring. She tugged off her glove, and he slipped it onto her finger, then squeezed her hand. "I'd much rather spend my life with you, no matter where we live."

Joy flooded her insides, so light and buoyant she thought her heart might float right out of her chest. She shrugged, mischief sparking from the happiness. "Honeymoon on Isle Royale?"

He grinned, his teeth gleaming in the light from the building, then pulled her in close. "Come here, you."

She leaned against him, her face tilted up, and their lips met in a soft kiss that held the promise of all the hope and joy of a lifetime of love together.

* * * * *

If you enjoyed Treacherous Escape,
be sure to check out
Dangerous Desert Abduction
by Kellie VanHorn

Available now from Love Inspired Suspense!
Discover more on LoveInspired.com

Dear Reader,

Thank you for braving the cold waters and rugged coastline of Lake Superior with Hudson and Vienna. Their story came to me as I was brainstorming national park settings for upcoming books. Why not choose one in my own state of Michigan? With its limited accessibility and minimal visitor resources, Isle Royale is one of the least visited national parks in the lower forty-eight states. There are no cars or roads on the island, and it is only accessible by boat or sea plane—making it truly a remote, natural paradise!

I love how God's handiwork is reflected in His creation for all to see, as it says in Romans 1:20. Both Vienna and Hudson find solace in nature after the heartaches they've endured, and they learn to look for God's goodness as He works all things together according to His plan. Just like them, I take comfort knowing that the sovereign Creator of all things loves us personally, so much that He sent His Son to die in our place. Through Him, we are more than conquerors!

My prayer for you is that you will find comfort and strength in His promises today. I love hearing from readers, so please feel free to get in touch. You can find me on my Facebook page (Kellie VanHorn, Author) or subscribe to my newsletter at www.kellievanhorn.com.

Warm regards,
Kellie VanHorn